BASTALAYO

The Assignment

Brooklyn L. Frazier

ISBN: 0998786403
ISBN 13: 9780998786407
Library of Congress Control Number: 2017907530
brooklyn frazier, Phoenix, AZ

Dedicated to my wife, Morrell

ACKNOWLEDGEMENTS

First and Foremost, I Thank God, My Lord and Savior Jesus Christ for blessing me with everything needed to complete this work.

In my journey writing and creating this book, I've discovered not everyone can see or get on board to one's dream. But Thank God, that he provides some around us that do and are true to the end. These are my very special people.

To my family whom without their love, support and belief in me, this book wouldn't have been completed. To my children and their spouses for their encouragement and confidence in my ability to finish the course. To my ten grandchildren and two nieces who inspire me daily and make me stronger. To my in-laws, Mr. & Mrs. Campbell and sister-in-law Sonja Campbell for unwavering belief in me. To my three brothers and sister who never doubted me. To my, Pastor Robert Johnson who inspired me and taught me regularly to believe big and don't put limits on what I can do in God. To Kendra Johnson, my daughter, who always believed in me and supported my dream investing with her professional help of editing, re-editing and reviewing the book. To my wife, Morrell, my soul mate and partner for life, co-writer, the one that had to bare the constant re-runs of my thoughts on this endeavor. Who contributed so much to the story and creation. To my friend's family and business associates (Subject Matter Experts). You provided the information to get the facts right to make the story real and believable. To Chris Lechuga: a true American soldier, friend, brother and with me from the very beginning, an intricate and important part of this journey. Michael Walden for your creative contributions and vital information. Ed Clark for your vital facts and information. Bradley Frazier, you invested in me out of the love in your heart. Larry Frazier, you read the book six times to help clean it up. Richard Frazier -you always provided vital information and historical facts. Stella Blake & Robert Broaddus, without hesitation supported my projects, always willing to be a help. Thanks to CS editor Chris for an amazing job. To all the un-named friends that helped me along the way. You know who you are. Thank You

BEFORE BASTALAYO

After Ed returned from his last mission in Iraq, eight months passed before he received his next assignment. He was to go to Bastalayo, where he would remain for six months to protect the family members of the ambassador of St. Vincent and the Grenadines. St. Vincent lay in the Caribbean Sea and was made up of volcanic rock and forests, as well as an abundance of streams that raced through the terrain. The people mostly were of African descent and were Caribbean. Their economy depended on the export industry, on such agriculture items as bananas and arrowroot. The other main economic resource was tourism. During Ed's stay, the ambassador would be working with the Americans who had been assigned to Bastalayo to increase the financial stability throughout the smaller island countries.

Ed figured he would get plenty of time to relax and enjoy the island. He saw no signs that this assignment would become a crazy web of mystery and corporate corruption, that the personal agendas would lead to tragedy and murder.

CHAPTER ONE

Day One: Sunday, the Flight to Bastalayo

In early May, Sergeant Ed Miller boarded a plane at the Miami International Airport and headed to Barbados. From there, it would take just another hour to fly to Bastalayo, an island territory of the United States, which lay in the Caribbean. Ed was a government special agent who handled a variety of assignments, and he was often sent around the globe to accomplish them.

Being six feet two, weighing 191 pounds, and having a 6 percent body fat, Ed was close to physical perfection. Raised in Philadelphia by African American parents, he came from a lineage of soldiers that led back to his great-great-great-grandfather, Akan Acu, who was an African slave from Durham, North Carolina. Acu went off to fight in the Civil War for the Union army to win his freedom. From that point on, every man from every generation in the Miller lineage fought in an American war, as did many other African Americans.

The plane was filled to capacity with open seating, but Ed was fortunate to get a window seat toward the front of the plane. After takeoff, a young flight attendant grabbed a microphone and gave the usual safety instructions. After she finished, she looked at Ed and smiled and hinted that she was interested in him. To receive such attention from pretty women was not unusual for Ed. They sensed something deeper than his good looks and easy confidence—they sensed the tiger in him, and the combination of his looks and that inner lethality made him into a lady's magnet.

He smiled back but turned his thoughts toward what lay ahead. Bastalayo was a large and beautiful island known for its warmth, its friendliness, and its variety of adventurous activities. It was about the geographical size of Hawaii. Also, it was renowned for how it affected people romantically. Ed reminded himself that his trip was about a mission assigned to him by the one he called Chief. Though he had not been given all the details of it, he did know that it involved protecting someone highly important to the government. Compared with his last assignment in Iraq, this mission should be a piece of cake, so he planned to take advantage of the simplicity and to enjoy his time there.

After twenty minutes aboard the flight, refreshments were served, and Ed ordered a Jameson on the rocks. The flight attendant handed him the drink and a bag of peanuts. While sipping the Jameson, he looked out the window at the clouds and reflected on how he had gotten to this point in his life. How, from an early age, he had always wanted to see the world and be a soldier. Reality had not turned out to be as glamorous as the dreams he had as a child—just the opposite, actually. Reality had been brutal and merciless, doling out heaps of mental and physical pain. Still, he would do it all over again; he believed that God had given him the grace to be this warrior so that he could fight for his love of his family and country.

A bell sounded, and the flight attendant made the announcement that the plane would be landing in five minutes. The bell's interruption took Ed from his thoughts, and he focused on what would happen after landing in Barbados. To reach the island of Bastalayo would take one more hour.

The island came into view at about six in the evening. As the plane approached its destination, Ed looked out the window and thought, "Man, this is going to be great—blue skies, deep-blue water, sandy beaches. This can be a sweet time."

The pilot announced that the plane would land in five minutes. The plane made its descent and then landed and pulled up to the boarding gate. The door opened, and as Ed stepped off the plane, there was a certain unique feel to the place, a feeling he had never felt anywhere else. A sense of excitement came over him, and he thought, "Yeah, this is going to be great."

Ed caught a cab and headed to the hotel. It was Sunday evening when he checked into the Buerada Hotel. His room was on the fourth floor and overlooked the pool. The sun was now going down, and he gazed out the window, his eyes focusing on a young couple playing in the shallow end of the pool, hugging and kissing as if they had not a care in the world. "Looks like love," he thought. He reflected upon his own life: "I was in love once. I've known lust many times…ahhhh!" Love, for him, was a different story. He wondered whether he could trust a woman with his heart again. He took one last glance at the couple, turned from the window, and poured himself a drink from the bar, which was in the corner of the room; then he undressed and took a quick shower. "Tomorrow is a big day—better hit it early," he told himself. Soon he was sound asleep.

CHAPTER TWO

Day Two: Monday

The next morning came quickly. "Better look the part today," he thought. Ed pulled a savvy black suit from the closet, along with a pressed white shirt and tie. His shoes were patent leather and had a military shine. In general, Ed dressed to impress as a way of life, which he learned during his upbringing on the East Coast.

He left his room, and as he passed through the hotel's lobby, he stopped off at the reservation desk. "Any messages for Ed Miller?" he asked.

A middle-aged woman in her midfifties said, "No, Mr. Miller, nothing here."

He told her thanks, and then he turned and walked out of the hotel and got a cab.

The cabbie made a sudden left-hand turn after fifteen minutes of driving, and Ed spotted his destination up ahead: 332 Othello Street, the army's headquarters. When the cab arrived, he stepped out of it, and two men hustled into it from the opposite side. The cabbie seemed delighted that he had another fare so quickly. Ed glanced at him and gave him a look that said, "Hey, you're on a roll!"

The cabbie smiled and said, "The fare is fourteen dollars and sixty-five cents."

Ed pulled out a twenty-dollar bill and handed it to him. "Keep the change," he said. He noticed that the young men in the cab were gabbing about an incident that happened in the coffee shop they had just left. They were saying something about an American woman who had been extremely rude to the cashier. Had either of them been the cashier, they said, they would have put the woman in check.

"Wow!" Ed thought. "Why do we Americans always get bent out of shape about everything?"

The army's HQ was a historic piece of architecture. It was three stories high, and its window sills, doors, and roof skyline had been painted with shades of tan colors. Two huge oak trees stood directly in front of the first floor's main windows, one on each side of the main entrance. The trees displayed a powerful sense of security. They looked strong enough to deter someone from crashing into the building with a car or truck.

Inside the building, old English artwork from the medieval era covered the walls of the building's first level—symbols, designs of swords and shields, and men of war dressed in full armor. The entrance's doors were made of old English oak. Some of the décor illustrated particular events; in particular, the scene next to the left of the entrance got Ed's attention. It displayed two knights jousting to the death. Their lances pointed toward each other, and their stallions were charging with no restraint. In the next scene, the lance of the knight on the larger stallion pierced through the heart of his opponent. As the beaten knight fell from his mare, he grabbed hold of his adversary's lance.

The scene led Ed to think about the fallen soldiers that he had seen in his time—those men and women in Afghanistan and Iraq, those on both sides of the battles. He too had been in that fallen state not too long ago. Luckily, he survived. The soldier on the wall, however, did not seem to be as lucky.

Being a soldier was the life Ed chose. When he entered the MPF building, he knew what to expect; he had been in such buildings many times before. The first floor housed the military's personnel files and finance operations, and the mailroom was there as well. The third floor was vacant and shielded from any signals or transmissions. The second floor was where he needed to go; he would get his operation orders there.

Ed approached the information desk, where he greeted a private. "I'm Sergeant Ed Miller," he said, "and I'm here to see Major Lewis."

The NCO used his computer to confirm Ed's appointment. "Yes, sir, have a seat." He called someone on a phone. Soon, a female officer came from one of the rear offices.

"Hello, Sergeant. I'm Lieutenant Ericson. The major was called away, so I will be the one to brief you. Please, follow me."

They walked up a staircase to the second floor. "I hope your trip here has been a pleasant one," said Ericson, making light conversation, trying to fill the dead air.

"Uneventful, you know. Good flight in, nice accommodations," replied Ed.

They reached the second floor; then they passed through another oak door, which was freshly painted with a soft-gray color and blended with the surrounding off-white walls. Upon entering the next room, which was the briefing room where Ed would get his operation orders, he saw a large vault in the center of the room. In front of it sat a huge, muscular soldier at a desk. His guns—that is, his arms—spread about nineteen inches, and when he stood up, he had to be about six feet six. He was a good-looking kid in his twenties and had a no-nonsense look on his face. Ed humorously whispered to the lieutenant, "I don't want to tangle with this guy!"

Lieutenant Ericson gave a smart chuckle and said, "I'll need you to place your phone and other articles in the basket before we go in." Her request was unnecessary: Ed was already relinquishing his phone and other items because he was so familiar with that drill.

They entered the vault and sat at a table that had two chairs set around it and a computer on top. Lieutenant Ericson turned it on and then entered a password. She pulled out a folder and handed it to Ed and said, "Here is a profile of your team; please, get familiar with them. Your mission will be to protect Ambassador Sydney Ballantyne of St. Vincent, along with his family. There have been threats against them recently. We suspect the threats must have something to do with the offshore-drilling rights. Since then, the United States has turned its sights to implementing alternative sources of power and to using oil from the United States' oil fields and from the Caribbean Sea. Caribbean countries have been scrambling to get in on the action. There's some nasty politics going on down here. The major players are BP, Mobile, Continental Resources Inc., Chevron, and Royal Dutch Shell—all of them are angling to get the oil rights for St. Vincent. There are a few others." Ericson paused, waiting for Ed to respond.

"Who are the others trying to get the oil rights?" Ed asked.

"They are some of the smaller Caribbean countries, and they have a lot to gain if the deal goes south. We suspect the threats are coming from them. As you know, St. Vincent's economy depends heavily on exporting its crop of bananas and on its tourism. The economy has taken a big hit during the last few years: the crops have been severely damaged by the increased hurricanes in the Caribbean. Scientists say the weather is due to global warming, and they anticipate things getting worse.

"The economy's second problem is that the countries tourism has been bashed with bad reviews stemming from the international fake news. False news reports have spread throughout social media. As much as we can tell, St. Vincent is being demonized by the competition through fake websites. Thus, this offshore oil contract is a big deal. Now, you are to meet Ambassador Ballantyne on Monday at the embassy on Delvo Affairs Boulevard."

Ed interrupted the lieutenant. "I'd like to bring in one of my own, someone I trust."

"I don't see a problem with your request, Sergeant, but he must pass our qualifications, and I will need to run your request by Major Lewis."

"Excellent," Ed said.

Equipment organized on a wall caught Ed's eye, and he assumed it was for him—a pair of night-vision goggles, a bulletproof vest, a government-issued cell phone (which would be linked directly to his teams' phones), a 9 mm Smith & Wesson automatic with six fifteen-round clips, and a few other gadgets.

Ed finished up with the lieutenant and left the building. A cab approached, and he flagged it down. Ironically, it was the same driver who had brought Ed there. "Hello again, sir," said the cabbie.

Ed echoed his greeting: "Hello again. I'd like you to drive me around and to show me some of the island."

"With pleasure! Do you want a tour? I can show you the beaches or maybe the shopping district or maybe some of—"

"No, not the tourist stuff, something or somewhere I can get a feel or pulse for the everyday life here."

Ed spent the next few hours exploring the island.

CHAPTER THREE

Day Three: Tuesday

The third day was uneventful, and Ed found himself relaxing by the pool, making phone calls, and trying to get into the soccer game displayed on the bar and grill's LCD screen. In between phone calls and sports news, he indulged in a little girl watching. After drinking two Jack and Cokes, he was feeling pretty good. A couple of girls strolled by. One was a blonde; the other was a brunette. Checking them out, he thought, "Nice eye candy." An older couple appeared. The man had a pot belly, as did the woman, but they seemed happy and in the moment. He looked over and saw Ed observing them, so Ed lifted his glass toward him and shouted, "Viva Bastalayo." The man nodded back and resumed his in-the-moment bliss.

Day Four: Wednesday
The early Bastalayo sun broke into the morning, glistening in a soft bluish-white color. It was 5:07 a.m., and light was piercing through

the beige curtains that covered one side of Ed's room, finding its way to the pillows on his bed and slowly across his face. Ed opened his eyes and squinted at the light welcoming him to the new day. The alarm on his Omega watch went off at 5:10 a.m., and he rose to go running, as he did every morning. He put on his workout gear and running shoes and headed out for a five-mile jog. The day before, the concierge was nice enough to map out a good path for him to take.

When he entered the lobby, he noticed a woman standing behind the reservation desk, but she was not the same one from the day before. No, the first woman was older, perhaps in her fifties, and she had a tint of gray in her hair and had a brown complexion; that lady was a full-figured.

The new woman before Ed was an eye-catcher. Her hair was short and of a fine grade; it danced mildly whenever she moved. Her back was toward Ed, so he watched her as she filed papers on a shelf. He saw her neck between the collar of her hotel uniform and her soft, dark hair. It was a dainty and shapely and beautiful little tower that led to the borders of her hairline, where her lovely earlobes radiated the glory that only a woman could display. She had an olive complexion and stood about five feet seven. If what was seen from behind was a sign of what was in the front, she would have to be an angel. When she turned around, it was confirmed: she was an angel—an angel that obviously worked out. She was strong and shapely in all the right places.

Her name, as displayed on her name tag, was Crystal.

"Good morning," she said.

"Good morning," Ed replied, walking up to her. "I'm Ed Miller, and I'm staying in room 423. Is there any mail for me?"

"Ah yes, Mr. Miller, there is one letter," she said, handing the letter over to him.

Ed could not resist the opportunity to flirt, being so pleasantly surprised by her beauty: "I have heard the mornings here were beautiful, but what I heard fell short of the reality. I am continually surprised by the things I'm discovering..."

She gave a light smile. "Aren't you the charmer. Perhaps you should go outside and see just how beautiful they are first."

Ed leaned on the reservation desk. "Oh, there's time enough for that. Are all the ladies here as pretty as you?"

She paused, feeling a little flirtatious and humorous, then responded with a low, slow, sensuous tone: "No, Mr. Miller, only the island's goddesses."

Ed laughed. "That's good; I'm sorry," he said. "I couldn't resist the opportunity to ask." He looked again at her name tag, which was pinned above a pocket on her blazer, and saw the word *manager.* "Allow me to start over. I'm Ed Miller, and you are?" he asked, hoping she would give him her whole name.

"Crystal, Crystal LeBlanc."

Feeling a connection, he said, "Nice to meet you. I'll be staying here for a while, but I don't know anyone here. Maybe you could tell me about some of the interesting things about the island over a cup of coffee?"

She looked at him inquisitively. Although she did not seem to be buying his lines, she did seem to acknowledge how good looking he was. Her eyes scanned his physique, seemingly pleased with what she saw.

The Miller charm had worked again.

She said, "I'll give it some thought."

He smiled. "Yeah, I hope you do." He turned and headed toward the lobby's front door.

"Nine thirty!" she said.

Ed stopped and turned around.

"Nine thirty—that's when I take my breaks. Come at that time."

He smiled and nodded, letting his eyes linger for an extra moment, and then he turned and left the lobby.

CHAPTER FOUR

Running down the main boulevard, he headed east and into the rising sun. The area was truly beautiful. However, the sunlight was a little blinding, and the morning motorists dreaded driving during that time of the day. Ed thought, "I should have brought my sunglasses. I'll be sure to wear them tomorrow." He ran about a mile, taking in the sights of the local stores and businesses, none of which were open yet, and he soon came upon the beginning of a residential area.

The houses were modest in size at first, varying from two- to five-bedroom homes. The homes' outer décors comprised colorful blues, yellows, and pinks, and many were two-story buildings. Almost every yard was well manicured, and many yards had tropical trees that were reaching to the rooftops and leaning toward the east, as though bowing to the sun.

After Ed ran another mile, he came across a park. Cutting through it, he saw a lake that covered about two acres and was filled with ocean water. Certain smells revealed that there were clown fish, blue devils, and tangs swimming around the surface. A bridge crossed the lake's center, and tall trees were planted along the northern shore. Beyond the trees was a hill, where several large homes sat. There were mansions and were very colorful like the homes Ed had already passed.

As with most islands, bright colors were expanding across the landscape. Ed took in these colors and the view as a whole. He was running "in the zone," and up ahead a man was running in the same direction. He was moving much faster than Ed was, so Ed caught up to him quickly and passed him. "Good morning!" Ed said.

"Yes, it is!" he chirped.

Ed picked up his pace. "Darn good speed," he thought. He had missed a few days of running and had been wanting to get in some good cardio.

He saw a dirt path that cut through two large houses up ahead, and he made a beeline for it. Holding a solid six-minute-mile pace, he spotted what appeared to be a body against the outer wall of one of the houses. At first Ed thought it was a homeless person sleeping, but something did not feel right. No, not at all. The twist in the body's legs signified that some kind of trauma had occurred.

Ed stopped to investigate—sure enough, it was a dead body. It was a white man with a well-groomed head of blond hair, dressed in a black V-neck shirt and black wrangler jeans. Ed placed the man's age in the late thirties. Dry blood was on the front of the dead man's face; it had flowed down from between his eyes to the side of his head. Upon closer evaluation, Ed saw the exit point in the upper-back portion of his head, again seeing blood. Looking around, Ed spotted a 9-mm casing, and he turned to see whether anyone else was around. No one else was in sight, except for the one jogger he had passed on the path. The jogger was disappearing in the distance, heading away from Ed.

In most countries, either 911 or 112 could be dialed to reach emergency services. Ed called 911.

"Nine-one-one. What is your emergency?" said a lady. Her voice was low in tone and tinged with a French accent.

"I discovered a dead body here in the park."

"Are you currently in danger?"

Ed told her no, but then it dawned on him that he did not know the name of the park, because the entrance sign, was covered over with vegetation, and the woman who had mapped out the running path simply called it, the park. He said, "I'm not from here and don't know the name of the park, but it's a mile north of the Buerada Hotel, in downtown Bastalayo. There's a large lake in its center. Do you know it?"

"Yes, I know it—St. Donte's Park. Can you tell me what side of the park you are on?"

Ed looked up at the sun, which was now rising in the east at about 0700. The body was lying to the left of the rising sun. "We are at the northeast end of the park, behind a large, turquoise-colored mansion. There are two large red homes directly east of us."

"We have someone on the way. Is there a number that we can reach you at? And what is your name?"

Ed gave her his name and his cell's number.

"You can hang up now; someone is on the way."

Being careful to avoid disturbing any evidence, Ed scanned the area a second time to see if there had been a struggle. "Could the man have come from one of these houses? Had he been taking a shortcut home through the park? Had this happened last night when there could have been other people present to see it? Had he been mugged? But then who would shoot a man between the eyes after mugging him?" wondered Ed. There was no sign of struggle, so he looked for other clues and spotted footprints near the 9-mm shell. At least three sets other than the deceased. Ed was not a cop, but he could see how this scenario played out.

The police had not yet arrived, but Ed did hear sirens off in the distance. Taking advantage of the time, he studied the direction of the footsteps, which headed back across the park toward downtown. The bulge in the man's back pocket showed that his wallet was still there, but before Ed could inspect it, the police arrived.

"Stand back, sir," one of the officers said. The officer approached cautiously with his hand on his gun; with his other hand, he signaled Ed to carefully move away from the body.

His partner was a few steps to the side of him, a hand on his gun as well, scanning the area around Ed, looking to see if anyone else was present. "Are you the one who called in the dead body?" he asked.

"Yes, officer."

"Do you have a gun?"

"No, officer."

Ed saw the name on his badge—Trenton. After assessing that the area was clear, the officers removed their hands from their guns. Ed heard the sound of another siren, this time coming from an ambulance. People were starting to appear in the park—some were jogging, some were walking their dogs, and some were just walking—and the flash of police lights grabbed their attention, making them curious to see what had happened.

Other officers arrived, and they proceeded to tape off the crime scene. Officer Trenton said, "Sir, we will need to take a report from you. Our detectives are on the way."

About that time, a man dressed in plain clothes and a woman in an all-black suit walked up. "Hello, I am Detective Wilson Williams, and this is Detective Stella Kaboo, and you are?"

"Ed Miller."

"Well, Mr. Miller, I understand that you were the first to find the body."

"Yes."

Wilson said, "Did you see anything or anyone when you entered the park, anything out of the usual?"

"There was a man jogging, but he veered off in another direction. There was no one else."

"Could you describe him?"

"He was about five eleven and maybe one hundred ninety pounds. He had fair skin but no hair, and he was wearing a light-green running outfit. I would guess that he is in his late twenties or early thirties. He appeared to be in very good shape."

"You were very observant, Mr. Miller. What time did you discover the body?"

Ed thought for a moment, for he had not brought his watch (he never did when he ran; he relied on his cell phone for the time). Then he remembered he had found the body right before he made the 911 call. He checked his phone log. "Five fifty-five this morning. Yeah, five fifty-five."

"What else did you notice?" asked Detective Williams.

"Nothing else."

The detective used a pad and pen to jot down the information. Meanwhile, Detective Kaboo was taking pictures of the body, working alongside another plainclothes officer, bending over the body, a pen in hand. She then crouched where the 9-mm shell lay and looked at the body; she seemed to be imagining the scene in her head, trying to figure out how this murder might have happened. She pulled the wallet from the dead man's back pocket and looked inside. Some cash was sticking out. She placed the wallet in a plastic bag that the other detective held open.

By then, quite a few people were surrounding the yellow tape; one uniformed cop was telling them to step back. Ed could hear chatter from the crowd. "Umm," he thought, "perhaps the killer had returned to the scene of the crime and was watching." He asked Detective Williams, "Are we done? Can I go now?"

"Sure, Mr. Miller, but I'll need to know where you are staying and your cell number, in case we need to talk to you again."

"I'm staying at the Buerada Hotel, room 423, and my cell is…" Ed gave his number and waited for the detective to say he could leave.

The detective recognized the area code. "Arizona, nice place. I was there once, went to see the Grand Canyon. What is the name of that town with the red rocks?" he asked.

"Sedona."

"Ah yes, Sedona. Thank you, Mr. Miller. Here, take my card; if anything else comes to mind, please call me. Have a nice day," he said.

With that, it was over. Ed cut his run short and went straight back to the hotel. He grabbed a bottle of water from the lobby and took a glance over at Ms. LeBlanc. The words just flowed from his lips: "Wow, really nice."

CHAPTER FIVE

I t hit Ed that he had not called Marrio Sanchez, his army buddy, since Ed got to the island. He spoke to his iPhone, telling it to call Marrio. It only took two rings when a voice came on

"Hola!" said Marrio.

"Hola! What's up, brother? How are you?"

Marrio was excited to hear from Ed. They were tight, as tight as two brothers could be. They joined the armed forces at the same time. Marrio came from San Antonio, and Ed came out of Philadelphia. They went through boot camp together and served together in Afghanistan once and in Iraq twice. Ed could trust his life to Marrio—whether Ed was in the trenches or anywhere else, for that matter.

Ed said, "I'm having a crazy day, man. You're not gonna believe this: I was out running and found a dead body."

"What in the hell! Did I just hear you say you found a dead body?"

They paused for a second. It was surreal, even though they were used to seeing bodies: they had seen them often on war tours, in the battlefields. But this killing had happened in Bastalayo, at a place on a tropical island, at a place filled with tourists and pretty beaches—at a place with a low crime rate. Ed broke the silence: "Yeah, look, maybe my karma is attracting this mess. I wonder what's next."

"So, did you call the cops?" asked Marrio.

"Yeah, they took a full report and asked me to get back to them if I thought of anything else I might have missed."

"Are you all right, man?"

"Yeah, I'm good. By the way, how's the family?"

"Everybody is doing fine. Pops is thinking about retiring and spending more time with my mom at the church. He's talking about giving the ranch responsibility over to Sergio, my younger brother. And my mom, well, you know she's real busy at the church. I swear that woman is a saint. I don't know how I came from her womb."

"Hey, you're a good guy," Ed said. "You do a lot for our country. You've put your life on the line a bunch of times, and you've got a good heart. I thought your dad wanted you to take over the ranch, though."

"He did and still does, but he knows I can't settle down in one spot. I've got a lot of this world left to see; maybe I'll take on the ranch some day, but definitely not now. Hey, how are the ladies down there? I know you have checked them out!"

"Well, so far so good—I must say the scenery is nice," Ed said, thinking about Crystal LeBlanc. "You'll have to come and see for yourself."

CHAPTER SIX

After checking the time on his phone, Ed saw that he was running tight on time. "Look, Marrio, I've got to run; I've got a meeting this morning. I'll call you later."

"Okay, brother, be safe" he said, and they both hung up.

Thoughts of the dead man flashed through Ed's mind. Thinking about the scene, he remembered the female detective had retrieved the man's wallet, and it had cash in it—so the man's murder probably did not result from a robbery. Detectives Williams and Kaboo had seemed to acknowledge to one another that there was something peculiar about that case. Ed wondered if there was more to the murder than it being a random homicide, more to it than the detectives let him know.

Ed forced the murder from his mind, and he ran up to his room, jumped in the shower, took a quick shave, and got dressed.

Ed had a nice, gray suit that he had purchased in New York, from down in the garment district. It was his business suit whenever he had to attend an official meeting. He told himself that he was going to step it up a notch with his next suits, maybe get some

Gieves & Hawks. That company's suits ran about two grand. Well, that might be a little much for his job but not for his night life. He liked dressing nice.

He put on a pair of Oxfords that he kept for these occasions, and he had a less expensive version of an Armani Collezioni black shirt. (The originals usually went for $275 or more.) His phone rang, and he answered it as he headed out the door. "Hello?" he said.

The voice on the phone was very pleasant. "Hello, I'm trying to reach Ed Miller."

"You've reached him. Who's asking?"

"This is the office of Ambassador Sydney William Ballantyne of the Grenadines, and we wish to confirm your appointment with his Aide, Clarence Dupont this morning."

"I will be there. We are scheduled for 10:00 a.m., right?"

"That is correct. We will see you then," she said. Realizing he would not be able to meet Ms. LeBlanc for coffee, he dialed her extension getting her answering machine. Ed left a message that something had come up, apologizing that he could not meet her for coffee at nine thirty, and that he would contact her later.

He then got on the elevator and pressed the button for the lobby. When he entered the lobby, he looked for the concierge, hoping to get directions to the government district. Ed noticed a man standing at the small Starbucks kiosk. He had been at the park that morning, had stood in the crowd of people during the investigation. Ed got a strange vibe from the man, his gut instincts telling him that something about the man was wrong. Ed shook the feeling off and kept things moving. He needed to focus on his meeting with the ambassador. Ed's job was to protect the ambassador and his family, and as far as Ed was concerned, doing his duty was where he would focus all of his attention. He needed to learn all the details of the ambassador's habits, anything that might put the man at risk. Ed needed to be thorough to keep the ambassador and his family safe.

CHAPTER SEVEN

Day Five: Thursday

Detective Kaboo slid a cup of black coffee in front of Detective Williams. Leaning over his shoulder, she looked at his computer screen, which displayed the mug shots of criminals who had just been released from prison. "Have you come up with anything?" she asked, scanning the profiles.

"Not yet, but we have to start somewhere, and this is as good a place as any," replied Detective Williams.

"What about forensics? Did they find anything?"

"They said the time of death was one in the morning, and the angle of the shot was directed upward—seems like our shooter was shorter than the victim, or was holding the gun low, and pointed it up when firing. Judging by the impression of one pair of footprints, they believe the shooter is five five. They're unsure whether the shooter is male or female."

"Perhaps the neighbors heard something or saw something," said Detective Kaboo.

"Yea, maybe a dog barking or someone up late watching television," said Detective Williams, nodding his head.

"I'll check with the neighbors."

"Wait. What about that witness? Do you think he was giving us straight answers?"

"Yeah, he seemed on the up-and-up. What do you think he does for a living?"

"I'm not sure," said Detective Williams. "He looks military, with his hard eyes and good physique. His hair was definitely military cut. He seemed pretty cool for having just found a corpse."

Kaboo nodded. "I'm sure he's no stranger to death. Perhaps we should keep tabs on him for a while."

Williams agreed. Williams pondered over the third set of footprints they saw at the crime scene. It wasn't clear whether they were part of it, the area in general had many footprints being that it was in a normal traveled pathway, but these were the freshest. He picked up his pad and pen and jotted his thoughts down, then placed both back on the desk. They left the precinct together and headed to the residential district by St. Donte Park.

CHAPTER EIGHT

Day Six: Friday

I-10 was nearly empty, except for the freight trucks doing seventy-five miles per hour while driving their goods to El Paso and beyond. It was still dark; morning had not broken through yet, but dozens of jack rabbits lined up against the side of the road, not far out of the reach of the massive truck tires, watching the trucks go by. A person might wonder whether the rabbits were entertained by the fast-moving vehicles, with the monstrous roars and bright lights beaming in front of them. One rabbit foolishly dodged into the road and met with misfortune—there was a crunching and squishy sound as the behemoth truck rolled by. The spectators, at the sight of tragedy, took off into the wild.

A single headlight was approaching speedily, and its roar was just as monstrous as a truck. This vehicle had only two wheels rolling under its frame. It was a jet-black Harley with the name Hell Fighter written on its sides. Sergeant Marrio Sanchez, the Harley's rider, was heading to Arizona; he was just coming off a week's leave. He had received a call from base that advised him of a new assignment. This time he was going to Bastalayo, thanks to a direct request placed by Sergeant Ed Miller.

Sanchez was a man with a six-foot-one frame; he weighed 190 pounds, which was all muscle, and he had only 3 percent body fat. He was dressed in army gear and wore a black motorcycle helmet. "Doggone it—how did he pull this off?" he thought. "We just talked a few days ago. Why didn't he mention that he requested me?"

Day Seven: Saturday
THE WEEKEND HAD come, and Ed rose early in the morning as normal. The phone rang; after looking at the caller on the screen, he answered it. "Hola, Marrio. What's up?" Ed glanced at his Omega watch; it was five in the morning but eight in Phoenix, where Marrio was. Again, he asked, "What's on your mind? It's five right now. If I didn't know better, I'd think you called this early just to get back at me for getting you assigned out here."

"Yeah, I got my marching orders. I'll be there Monday. But I don't expect you're willing to tell me what's going on—though I'm hoping you might."

"No, not over the phone. The rundown will have to wait until you get here."

"Well, okay. So be it—Monday it is."

"So how is what's her name doing?" Ed asked. "The Tucson babe you were seeing."

Marrio grunted. "She's yesterday's news. We fell out over some crazy stuff.

"Like what?" Ed asked.

"She got bent out of shape because I wouldn't go out double dating with her girlfriend and her man. She was getting too possessive. One disagreement led to another, and before I knew it, we broke it off."

"Well, you know that you are not one to let grass grow under your feet. Whatever the case when you get here there will be enough pretty ladies to keep you busy. They are everywhere and fine."

"I hear you, Sarge, and I'm definitely looking forward to it. So what about you, player? Are you still celibate?" asked Marrio, starting to laugh.

"Oh, you've got jokes. Nobody right now. I'm still working on getting my head back in the game."

Eight months had passed since Marrio and Ed had returned from their last mission. Ed saw Kamari, a beautiful, promising model from LA, for at least two years, and he had been deeply into her and thought she had felt similar feelings, but a man can never really know what is inside a person.

When Ed was over in Iraq and under hellish conditions, the last thing he needed was emotional instability. Kamari texted a Dear John note, and Ed could not believe it. "I don't need this crap now," he had thought, getting real pissed. "Why would she do this now?" He had needed her support more than ever. She was one of the reasons why he fought; Ed had only wanted to protect his country, family, and the ones he loved. He felt hurt, betrayed, and confused. If Marrio had not been there to help him get through it, Ed would have made some bad mistakes out there in the war zone.

"That selfish little bit", Ed stopped in the middle of his thoughts, not wanting to get trapped spiraling down memory lane. "I'm trying to clean up my language, and dwelling on it will only screw me up," he thought. But what could he expect? She had been young and ambitious. In hindsight, he realized that she had the depth of a kids' pool. She was beautiful but had lacked substance. Even if Ed had known better, he still would have fallen for her. "All right, lesson learned," he thought.

"Ed? Ed? Are you there?"

"Sorry, man. I'm here. So, look, I'll see you when you get here. I'll pick you up at the airport."

"Okay, see you Monday."

CHAPTER NINE

Detective Kaboo knocked on the door of the large, turquoise mansion at which the corpse had been discovered. A short, Hispanic lady dressed in a black maid's uniform answered the door.

"Hola! Hablas English, senora?" asked Kaboo.

"Si, can I help you?" said the maid.

"We are looking for the owners of the home. Are they in?" asked Kaboo.

"Uno momento," said the maid before closing the door.

A moment later, a middle-aged French woman appeared. "May I help you?" she asked.

"I'm here to ask you a few questions about last Tuesday night. Are you aware there was a murder behind your home? The body was discovered early Wednesday morning, at about five thirty." Detective Kaboo looked intently at the woman as she answered.

"Yes, that is what I heard from my neighbors," said the French woman. "Unfortunately, I was not home that night; I was out of town on a business trip."

Kaboo continued her questioning: "What is your name?"

"Antoinette Balestra."

"And what line of work are you in?"

"I'm a consultant for Royal Dutch Shell."

"You said you were out of town during the incident—when did you get back?"

"Thursday morning, but you should speak with my house sitter: she was here during that time. Her name is Beverly, and I have her phone number."

"Thank you, Ms. Balestra. You said your neighbors mentioned the body to you. Did they happen to say whether they heard or saw anything unusual?"

During Kaboo's questioning Balestra, Detective Williams was revisiting the spot where the body had been found. Looking around, he noticed that the house to the left of the Balestra home had a pair of Dobermans. If the dogs had heard the shot, they surely would have barked, and someone would have awakened.

Standing about where the shooter would have been, Detective Williams could see a second-story window of the large red mansion; the window was between two large, tropical trees. The angle of the window to the shooter provided a clear view, and on Tuesday night, there was a full moon. If someone had woken and looked out of the window, that person would have easily seen the killer.

Williams then walked around to the front of the house and met up with Kaboo, who had finished questioning Ms. Balestra. "Did you find out anything?" asked Williams.

"Just that the homeowner, Ms. Balestra, was out of town during the murder, but she had a house sitter. I've got her info. What did you find out?"

"I'm not sure yet. I'd like to talk to the people in that red house."

The detectives approached the door, Williams leading the way. As he reached to knock, the door swung open, and a teenage boy darted out, startling the detectives. Instinctively, they reached for their weapons but quickly realized the kid was laughing. Another teenager, a girl, ran out behind him, and she was shouting, "I'm gonna get you, Jerome!"

The detectives looked at each other and took deep breaths to relax. "Okay," said Williams, "let's try this again." He rang the bell.

A woman answered this time. "May I help you?" she asked.

"Yes, I'm Detective Williams, and this is Detective Kaboo. We'd like to ask you some questions about the body that was discovered behind your neighbor's house Wednesday morning. What is your name, please?"

"Sylvia Rice," she said.

"Any relation to Condoleezza?" asked Williams.

"She is a distant relative, a second or third cousin on my husband's side."

Williams smiled. "She is a brilliant woman. May I call you Mrs. Rice?"

"Yes."

"Mrs. Rice, did you or your husband happen to see anything or hear anything late Tuesday night or around one o'clock Wednesday morning?" asked Williams.

"No, I don't remember noticing anything peculiar around that time; however, earlier—oh, about ten thirty at night—I looked out of my window and happened to see a man and a woman standing by a bench by the lake. Their presence grabbed me—there was something odd about them. Their body language seemed off. They looked too ridged and glanced around constantly." Mrs. Rice shrugged her shoulders, trying to recall more details. "What is more, hardly anyone comes to this side of the park at night."

Detective Williams asked, "Can you describe the man and woman?"

"Yes, they wore dark clothing. The woman was white. Her dark hair fell just a few inches below her shoulders. She was short, maybe five three. The man was a dark-skinned black and stood about six feet tall. He had a short Afro and wore a beard, not a long one, from what I could make of it—one of those short, gruff ones."

"Anything else, Mrs. Rice?" asked Detective Kaboo.

"No, that is all I can remember," she said.

Detectives Williams and Kaboo thanked the woman and left. "If that man and woman have something to do with the murder, then the woman was the shooter," said Kaboo.

"And the one calling the shots," added Williams. "We ought to have a name on the corpse by now. I'm pretty sure this was the same guy down at Delvo Affairs Boulevard, the one who showed up on the embassy's cameras."

"I've run photos of the suspects, by the FBI, just in case we don't come up with anything. We need to revisit the profiles again," said Kaboo.

They got into a dark-brown Impala SS and drove away.

CHAPTER TEN

Day Eight: Sunday

I t was Sunday, and the day was young, and Ed was up and heading out to enjoy his day off. After hailing the one cab that was parked outside the hotel, he told the driver to head to the beach. When the cab arrived, Ed saw that the beach was already two-thirds full of young, fleshy bodies showing off their beauty and brawn. Music loudly played from large speakers on the roof of the Umbrella and Beach Chairs shop. There were several boats out in the ocean. Many were pulling tourists parasailing and water skiing; others were connected to water-jet flyboards, which tourists used to dive in and out of the water. This was Corondo, the number one beach in Bastalayo. Being there was the equivalent to being in Jamaica or the Bahamas.

Ed looked to the left; about a mile down the beach, he saw the Bastalayo Casino, which stood forty floors tall. (At night, it would light up like a Christmas tree.) There was a slew of hotels to house tourists, partiers, and gamblers. To Ed's right were shops lined up along the beach and street, shops that were bars, food grills, and rental shops. There was a large stage for holding concerts and for hosting the island's cultural events.

Ed entered a straw market to his left to see if he could find something for his mom. He always picked something out for his mom whenever he traveled and sent the gifts back to her. His mom and dad lived in Philly. He was born and raised there, and it would always be home to him. His father and uncles served in the Vietnam War, and his mom held the family together when they were sent overseas into action. She had been through a lot, losing an uncle in the Korean War when she was a child; she remembered the sadness and her family's long recovery after the loss. Later, she had to live with the fear of losing her husband and brothers-in-law. She had to worry about Ed on three separate occasions: once in Afghanistan, twice in Iraq—who knows, maybe a fourth time, yet to come, in Iran, with the way things were going. Ed felt that such gifts were his way of letting her know that he was okay on his trips.

In the straw market, he walked through the aisles and saw the usual island souvenirs: Bob Marley shirts, tropical-island printed shirts, beaded jewelry, and so on. He stopped at one stand where a tall black man was sitting behind its table. He had a Hershey-brown complexion and sported a waxed bald head, some red shorts, a black-fishnet body shirt, and some black sandals.

As Ed looked over the table, the man asked, "What are you looking for?"

"I'm trying to find something unique, something different."

"Have you ever seen this?" he asked, handing Ed a figurine and statue of a man and woman on a beach. The woman was dancing barefoot on the sand; the man appeared frozen in awe at her presence, while the tide rippled up the sand, under a full moon in the backdrop. It was quite grabbing.

"What is it?" Ed asked. "Is it trying to express something meaningful?"

"It is a symbol of a love story, a myth we have here on the island. You see, Bastalayo nights are intoxicating and magical; under their spell, one finds it hard to avoid falling."

"Falling? You mean falling in love?"

"Yes, that is exactly what I mean, and many here believe the heavens have created this island just for that, to bring together some special hearts that must find each other—perhaps this might happen to you."

Ed thought about what the man said, for a few brief seconds, and then said, "You almost had me—good story, mister. But because you are so convincing, I'll take it."

"What's your name, soldier?"

"Is it that obvious?" Ed asked.

"Well, I'm pretty good at picking out people, and you fit the package."

"My name is Ed, and yours?"

"I'm Kwame."

Kwame was an interesting person. He had come down to the straw market to see his young entrepreneurial nephew, who owned the stand that Kwame was now watching. Kendrick, his nephew, had needed to step away for moment, so Kwame was watching the store for him. What Kwame actually did was run two very successful nightclubs, which he owned. One was an upscale jazz club called Xavier's Jazz Club, and the other, Cymbal's, was the hottest dance club on the island. Besides his businesses, he was well connected in the political arena and knew all the power players on the island.

Kendrick appeared. He shared his uncle's features and height; however, Kwame was well built, and the nephew had yet to fill out because he was still young. The nephew was about sixteen years old but seemed mature for his age. He then said, "Thanks Unc— I'm good now."

Kwame nodded to his nephew and then asked Ed, "Are you enjoying your time here?"

"I've been here about a week, and it seems really nice," Ed said, leaving the part out about the corpse he had found.

"Yes, Bastalayo is a very nice place, and the people are friendly and accommodating. But have you checked out the nightlife?"

Ed humorously thought, "Yeah, accommodating to everyone except Mr. Hole-in-the-Head lying in the park. He said, "No, I haven't yet; I've been busy checking out the daytime scenes."

Kendrick watched us converse and noticed that we were hitting it off well. Ed asked Kwame about things to do in town.

"I know several nice spots to check out in the evening, places at which I'm sure you will have a good time. As a matter of fact, this Friday there is a best-dressed contest down at Xavier's Jazz Club. The club is a very classy place, and the people stand out. Also, the ladies are incredible!" Kwame smiled, showing his big pearly whites, which seemed to light up the whole area.

Ed smiled back and said, "I am a fan of jazz, and dressing up is definitely one of my passions. You surely have my interest."

Kwame handed Ed his business card, which read Xavier's Jazz Club, A Taste of Class: 222 Mallow Avenue, Phone 555-321-6000. The card was black with gold lettering and borders, an eloquent design. Kwame Taylor's name was on the card as the owner.

Kwame then introduced Ed to his nephew. "And this is my nephew, Kendrick," he said.

"Cool," said Ed, "I'm glad to meet you. Yeah, I like how that jazz club sounds. Look, I'm staying at the Buerada hotel. We should hook up sometimes," he said to the both of them.

CHAPTER ELEVEN

Day Nine: Monday Morning

American Airlines flight 957 arrived at the Barrack Obama Airport, pulled up to the boarding deck, and opened its door. The passengers walked out. A well-built man with a tan complexion and jet-black hair exited the plane. A flight attendant standing at the exit door moaned mildly as he walked by, moved by his presence and charisma. Marrio Sanchez was finally in Bastalayo. After getting his bags (which were already at the carousel), he headed for the arrival curb.

Ed saw him curbside and called out, "Marrio! Good to see you brother."

"Likewise. Thanks for picking me up."

"Yeah, well, you know I've got to have my main man with me when I go into action," Ed said.

"So what's on the agenda, and where do I fit in?"

They walked to the garage parking and jumped into a new steel-gray Dodge Challenger. "Hey, there's some water in the back seat. Grab one, man," Ed said.

"No, I'm good. So what's up?"

"Our job is to protect Ambassador Sydney William Ballantyne of St. Vincent, who has received several death threats recently. HQ thinks the threats are serious, so they want us to keep him alive. What HQ has told me is that the heavy oil corporations are fighting over the offshore rights to St Vincent and that a few other neighbor territories have a lot to gain if the Grenadines are removed temporarily until they can get the deals. HQ put a team together for me, but I don't know any of them. I need you to have my back. I need to know there is someone who instinctively knows my process, so there won't be lag time when we go into battle mode. I trust you for that."

Marrio did not hesitate before he said, "Okay, you know I got your back."

"We have to go to the embassy and meet up with the ambassador. I'll get you to the hotel, so you can change in my room and check in later."

CHAPTER TWELVE

Back at the precinct, Williams and Kaboo were going over profiles of possible suspects.

"Call Kwok," said Williams, "and see if he has identified the corpse."

Kaboo dialed Officer Le Kwok's extension and waited for him to answer. "Le, this is Stella. What do you have for me?"

"We ran his prints and came up with a Dugan Metcalf. He was a private-contract engineer and did a lot of work with offshore oil rigs. His last employer was Mobile, the oil company," said Le Kwok.

"Thanks, Le. Send that info over to me."

"Sure thing, Stella" said Le, who then hung up.

"Our victim was a private engineer contracting in the oil business," said Kaboo "What was this guy doing in St. Donte Park on a late Tuesday night?"

"And what was he doing that ended up costing him his life?" asked Williams. "Let's check the surveillance cameras of the stores near the crime scene; maybe we'll get lucky and get a glimpse of our odd couple." He was referring to the potential suspects. "I'm going to call a guy I know over at Mobile and see if he can shed some light on this Dugan Metcalf."

ED AND MARRIO left the Buerada Hotel and headed to Delvo Affairs Boulevard to meet the ambassador. At the embassy, Ed parked in the rear parking lot, close to the building itself. They got out of the car, and Ed took a minute to observe the layout. He said, "We'll be watching him a lot from here. By the way, I left out the part that we are watching his two daughters as well."

"I understand that they are twins," said Marrio.

"I see you've done some homework. Let's get up there and meet our guy."

"What about the team?"

"Plenty of time for that this afternoon. We'll meet up with them at the air force base," Ed replied.

They entered the embassy and were directed to the ambassador's office. Ed knocked on the office door.

"Come in," said a man with a deep voice, which seemed to rattle the door.

They entered. The ambassador was not quite what they had expected. A man of African descent stood before them. He was about five feet seven and had a moderate frame. He wore a light-blue shirt with long sleeves and dark-brown trousers. He had hair but not enough to justify leaving it on his head. He should have shaven it all off, but perhaps he had vanity for the little he had left.

"Ah, Sergeant Miller," said the ambassador, sticking a hand out to shake Ed's. "And you are?" he asked, looking at Marrio.

"Sergeant Marrio Sanchez. I'm glad to meet you, sir."

"He is part of my team," Ed added, thinking that the ambassador must have been given their profiles, just as they had been given his "I would like to keep things simple," said the ambassador. "I am a very busy man, so I hope we can see eye to eye on everything, Sergeant Miller."

"Mr. Ambassador, we will do everything in our power to keep you and your daughters safe. We will have to lay down some ground rules, which we will go over with the three of you. What we will need from you is your full cooperation. We'll try to give you as much space as possible, but until we see just how assertive these attackers are, we will be close."

Ambassador Ballantyne sighed. "Sergeant—"

"Call me Ed, sir."

"Okay, Ed, I have lots to do, and I have to keep things moving—I often have to improvise at times. I don't see why your government feels that my life is in danger. Perhaps you can focus on guarding my girls and back off me somewhat. I'm sure I'll be okay." The Ambassador's daughters were twins, 15 years old, Shantel and Romara Ballantyne. They were supposedly a handful.

"No disrespect, Ambassador, but we've got a job to do. Unless my superiors change my orders, I will run a tight operation."

The ambassador stared hard at Ed. "I thought you might say that, Ed. Your people tell me you're the real deal. Okay then, Ed, we'll do it your way for now. I'll talk to your people again."

CHAPTER THIRTEEN

Detectives Williams and Kaboo approached Jonell's Men's Wear, which was on the corner opposite to St. Donte Park. Looking at the store's outside camera, they noticed that it angled toward the front entrance of the park. Inside the store, Kaboo approached the man behind the counter. "Hello, I'm Detective Kaboo, and this is my partner, Detective Williams. We are investigating a homicide that happened last Tuesday night and would like to review your surveillance tapes."

The man said, "Unfortunately, my cameras have been down the last two weeks, and we have been unable to get them fixed—we are still waiting on parts."

"That's too bad. We were hoping you could help us. Thanks for your time," said Kaboo.

"Let's try the jewelry store across the street," said Williams.

They headed across the street and opened the store's glass door. Inside, an older woman was standing in front of the cashier's counter. She was in her sixties and was wearing a gold dress slit down to her knees and matching high-heel shoes. Past her was an older man; he was sitting at a desk and examining gems.

"Hello, are you the proprietor?" asked Kaboo.

"No, that would be Mr. Black, the man back there," said the woman.

The detectives approached the man and introduced themselves. Kaboo said, "Mr. Black, we are investigating the homicide that happened in St. Donte Park, and we need to see your surveillance tapes from last Tuesday night."

"No problem, Officers. Last Tuesday night, okay," said Mr. Black. He walked into a back office and returned shortly with a tape. "Last Tuesday night, here you go, Officers. You can take it with you and drop it off when you're finished with it."

"Thank you, Mr. Black," said Kaboo.

Back outside, Williams said, "I'll go back across the street and see if there are any other surveillance cameras that might have picked up our suspects. I'll meet you back at the car when I'm done."

Kaboo nodded in agreement.

ED AND MARRIO wrapped up their meeting with Ambassador Ballantyne and headed to the Torren Air Force Base, which had just officially opened one year ago. There they would meet the team.

Dennis Rollins was a civilian contracted by the government for special assignments. He had a master's degree in computer science and was presently flirting with aerospace studies. He grew up in the hood in Inglewood, California. He started out at Los Angeles Community College and studied for about two years there; then he found his way to Silicon Valley and discovered that technology and data security suited him quite nicely. He had been the brightest in his class, so Uncle Sam took notice and recruited him. He got into an army contract via a specially designed program that solicited highly skilled techs for special missions.

Yolanda Hernandez was from New York City. She grew up in Spanish Harlem, joined the Army ROTC at fifteen, enlisted at eighteen in the army, and eventually decided to be a lifer. She specialized in tactical weapons and was a bomb specialist. Among other talents, she had a fifth-degree black belt in karate.

Randell Thornton was from Boise, Idaho. He grew up as a farmer and hunter. At nineteen, he joined the army to fight in Iraq. He served two tours, specializing in hand-to-hand combat and tactical weapons. He was working on a degree in agriculture and botany.

Then there was Marrio, who had a BA in psychology. During his time with Special Forces, he trained extensively with sniper training, tactical weapons and hand-to-hand combat, and received other special training. He served once in Afghanistan and twice in Iraq, completing dozens of special operations throughout the globe.

Ed's own resume, started after he joined the army at eighteen, include a Bachelor Degree in psychology and criminology, completion of the (PME)- Professional Military Education, studied Martial arts, Military Free-Fall Advanced Tactical Infiltration and Special Forces Training including tactical weapons and hand to hand combat. Ed, like Marrio, also served once in Afghanistan and twice in Iraq, completing dozens of special operations throughout the globe.

TORREN AIR FORCE BASE, being a new base, kept tight security. Ed drove the steel-gray Dodge Challenger up to the guarded entrance. A well-built soldier walked up to the driver's side. Ed stated his business and showed his military identification, and Marrio did the same. The guard went back to the guard shack and checked the identification with his computer and then made a call on the phone. After verifying the info, he looked at his counterpart and nodded. The other guard raised the gate with the push of a button. Ed drove to a multi-purpose-facility where the team was waiting. After Marrio and Ed entered the room, two of the specialists saluted them. Marrio and Ed saluted back, but Ed told them that from then on, they would not bother with formalities.

"I'm Sergeant Ed Miller, and this is Sergeant Marrio Sanchez." Ed looked at Dennis Rollins. "You specialize in computer technology and data security."

"That's right, sir. I can hack anything, find anything, and fix anything—computer related, of course. And I work fast," said Rollins.

"Can you do it under pressure?" Ed was being rhetorical, so he quickly held up a hand, not requiring or wanting an answer. "Okay, and you're Yolanda Hernandez; your profile is quite impressive. There was no mention of battle experience, though. Tell me, have you ever had to use your skills in any real situations?"

"No, sir. However, I did put a couple of rookie marines in their place, outside a bar in downtown San Diego. That was about two years ago. I also have had my share of karate tournaments as a black belt," said Hernandez.

"How did you fare in the bouts?" Ed asked.

"I won them all, except one, sir."

"Oh, what happened with that one?"

"He never showed up, sir. Word had it that he was scared of being beat by a woman," said Hernandez, glancing over to Marrio, who smiled, clearly amused by Hernandez's words and humorous expression.

Ed looked at the last member of the team. "You are Randell Thornton, and you have seen action twice in Iraq. Why did you join the army, son?"

"I love my country, sir. I wanted to fight for her."

"Have you ever killed a man?"

"Excuse me, sir?"

"Have you ever killed in battle?"

After pondering the question briefly, he said, "I don't know, sir. My battalion was in a few skirmishes; I fired my weapon at the enemy, but I don't know if I ever hit anyone. We never were right up on our targets, and our skirmishes seemed to occur mostly at night.

"If something should happen on your watch, I need to know I can count on you to make the tough call and make it quick."

After giving them the detailed operation info, Ed advised the team members on what their duties would be. After concluding the meeting, Ed looked at Marrio the way he did many times. Marrio intuitively knew exactly what Ed was thinking. Marrio left and headed to the administration building to get authorization to use the gym privately. They needed to test these soldiers to see if they would make the cut. There could be no mistakes; neither Marrio nor Ed could accept a single error.

CHAPTER FOURTEEN

Two thousand dollars was already in the pot of this intense no-limit Texas Hold'em game. A young Asian man made a quarter-sized pot bet, amounting to $500. The dealer—a very striking, vivacious brunette with a professional demeanor—looked at a plump, middle-aged blonde smoking a thin, long brown cigarette. "It's on you," said the dealer.

After a slight hesitation, the blonde said, "I raise." The players all became very attentive to the action. The woman was taking her time deciding on the amount. The tension at the table was quite palpable. Finally, the blonde said, "Make it sixteen hundred," cutting out the chips from her stack.

The young Asian man who had originally opened the betting looked and studied her face. She nonchalantly turned her head slightly upward and blew out the smoke from her cigarette, smiling meekly, giving away the fact that she had a strong hand. She then looked over at the man across from her. She was the only woman in the game. Two of the other older males folded. One of the other players left in the hand, a middle-aged male with graying hair, studied her carefully. His relaxed demeanor was not observed by the other players, particularly by his remaining two opponents. After about a minute, which seemed like an eternity to the woman, he stated, "I'll reraise." He stacked $5,150 on the betting line.

The woman's smile was replaced with quivering lips, the wrinkles around her eyes becoming more pronounced. The young Asian threw his cards into the muck. After deliberating for maybe ten seconds, she called the raise.

The dealer proceeded to ask her to reveal her cards. However, the gentleman who reraised should have shown his cards first, because the woman had called him. She did not challenge the dealer's request, only nervously turned over her cards, revealing kings full of deuces. The graying male turned his cards over— quad jacks. Ahhs emanated from the other players as they watched the dealer push a monster pot to the man.

Michael Klein, the winner, was one of the best—if not *the* best— poker players in Bastalayo. It was his favorite hobby. What he did for a living was manage a team of engineers and contractors of heavy-rig equipment in the oil industry.

The woman cashed out, as did Michael Klein. "That's it for me," said Klein to the dealer, giving her a substantial tip.

The dealer thanked him. "Good game, Mr. Klein. Have a nice night," she said in a warm tone.

Klein slid a few more bucks over to her, sweetening the tip a little. He always took care of the dealers as long as they did a good job controlling the game by keeping it moving fast and by making sure it adhered to the rules. She had made one mistake, but Michael did not hold that over her.

Looking at his phone, he saw that he had missed a call. He pushed the button that played his voice messages.

"Hello, Michael. This is Detective Williams at police HQ. I'd like to speak with you. I have a few questions to ask you about one of your previous contractors. Please, call me when you get this."

Klein hit the callback button and waited for Williams to answer.

"This is Detective Williams."

"Hey, Wilson. This is Michael Klein; you called about one of my contractors."

"Yes. Hi, Michael. Thanks for the prompt callback. I don't know if you're aware, but one of your previous contractors was murdered last Tuesday night, and I need to know whatever I can about the guy. His name was Dugan Metcalf."

"I was not aware; this is the first time I've heard about it," said Klein.

Williams knew Klein from the Bastalayo casino. He had watched some of the high-stake games that Klein played in and even cheered him on sometimes. He recognized Klein's brilliance with cards. Williams himself was a craps player, a small-bet player, but he still played with passion.

"Dugan Metcalf? Yes, I know him," said Klein. "We had a go-around, and I had to get rid of him. We could not fully prove it but strongly suspected that he was stealing confidential information and passing it on to our competition, Royal Dutch Shell. He talked fast and was elusive when we asked him questions. I never trusted that guy. Someone higher up got him into my organization, and I had little say in the matter. It doesn't surprise me at all that something happened to him."

"Why do you say that?"

"The guy knew his stuff but had a dark side to him. I don't think he developed any genuine working relationships while he was here. He always seemed as if he was after something, you know, pursuing some interior motive or a hidden agenda. How did he die?"

"A bullet between the eyes," said Williams.

"Poor fool—the kid was smart and had a lot going for himself. He was just too ambitious and impatient to wait for his blessings to develop."

"If you don't mind telling me, what did you have him working on?"

"Surveying and making blueprints for the southern side of St. Vincent's offshore areas for deep digging," said Klein, turning and watching the middle-aged blonde he had just beaten at the card table, who was smoking another of the thin, long brown cigarettes. She was leaving the casino.

CHAPTER FIFTEEN

Day Thirteen: Friday

The rest of the week went slow as the team and Ed settled into their routine. Friday came, and Ed assigned Hernandez and Thornton to cover the weekend security.

"Marrio! I'm going clubbing tonight. There's a jazz club that's supposed to be tight, and I'm going to check it out. Do you want to tag along?" Ed asked.

"I'll pass, man. I'm going to rent a bike and hit a few trails."

"Cool, I'll catch up with you later."

They took the elevator at the same time and entered the lobby of the hotel. Ed spotted Crystal LeBlanc at the reservation desk. She had been out of town on business, but now she was back and, perhaps, even more breathtaking. Ed motioned to Marrio. "Hey, check her out—two o'clock."

Marrio looked over and saw Ms. LeBlanc, and it was as if everything were moving in slow motion for Marrio. She was dressed in a fine-fitted business blouse and skirt and killer heels.

"Hey, let me introduce you to her," Ed said.

Crystal looked up from her work as they approached her. She looked at Ed and smiled before greeting them. "Good day, gentleman."

"Hello, Ms. LeBlanc," Ed said.

"Hello," said Mario, barely managing the two syllables.

Crystal noticed the glisten in Marrio's eyes, and she blushed a bit.

Ed caught on to what was happening. He looked at his friend and then back to Crystal. "So I haven't seen you all week."

"Yes, I've been away on business, but I'm back now. How was your week—exciting, I hope?"

"Actually, it was all business until today," Ed said.

She glanced again at Marrio. "What are your plans for the evening?" she asked casually.

Marrio seized the moment and joined the conversation. "A moonlight bike ride if I can find a motorcycle rental."

"I'm checking out Xavier's Jazz Club. I heard there is a best-dressed contest tonight, and I'm told it's a real nice event."

Crystal observed both men, wanting to make the most of the attention they were giving her. "Well, sounds as if you both are going to have fun. By the way, please call me Crystal."

Ed and Marrio assented.

"Crystal," Ed said, "you know we never got to have that coffee, since you were out of town and I had to set up for work. Would you consider going out with me tonight?"

"I'm flattered," she said.

Marrio followed by saying, "You know that an awesome ride on a motorcycle under the moonlight would be a lot of fun."

Crystal, seeing Marrio and Ed contending for her, basked in the attention. "Well, gentlemen, the offers are nice, but I will have to pass. I'll be working late tonight." The reservation desk's phone rang. "Have a nice day, guys. I do have to answer this," she said.

Marrio and Ed headed toward the front door. Marrio went across the lobby to the concierge. Ed pulled the black and gold business card from his wallet, the one for Xavier's Jazz Club, and dialed the number on the card. He waited for Kwame to answer.

"Hello, Xavier's."

"I'm trying to reach Kwame Taylor," Ed said.

"One moment please," said the voice.

Kwame soon answered. "Hello, this is Kwame Taylor. How may I help you?"

"This is Ed Miller; we met at your nephew's straw shop at the beach."

"Ah yes, Mr. Miller. How are you? Are you considering coming down to my club tonight?"

"Yes, I am. I'm flying solo, so what time should I show up?"

"Things start to pop about nine, so you should leave about fifteen minutes before then. I'll send a car around for you."

"You don't have to do that," Ed said.

"No worries, man. Let me do this. You're my guest tonight."

Ed thought Kwame was giving him special treatment out of respect for Martin, his younger brother, who was a marine killed in Iraq during the first invasions. Kwame had a special place in his heart for soldiers. "Okay, Kwame—you're on. At a quarter to nine, I'll be ready," Ed said and then hung up.

Marrio was talking with the hotel concierge, who was a young and bushy redhead. She looked like Mariah Carey in the face but was quite petite. She was wearing a pair of tan khakis, a white polo shirt, and red running shoes. She seemed to be a college kid. In her eagerness to help Marrio, she was fumbling across her desk and greeting him exuberantly. "Hi, how can I help you?" she asked.

It hit Marrio that he had approached Crystal with the same excited appearance. He cast prudence aside. "I'd like to rent a bike for tonight."

"Well, let's see what I can find for you…mister?" she said, waiting to get his name.

"Call me Marrio," he said.

"Marrio. Okay, Marrio," she said, exhaling a low groan of sensual appeal. "Let's see. There is Terrence Tours; they have ATVs, jeeps, and motorcycles for rent. They have Hondas, Yamahas, and a few Harley-Davidsons."

"That's great. Would you please call them for me?" asked Marrio, smiling at the young, enchanted girl.

She soaked up as much of his smile as she could, and then she dialed Terrance Tours and handed the phone to Marrio.

"Hi," said Marrio, "I'm looking for a Harley to rent tonight."

"We have several. I'm sure you'll find one you like," said the salesman confidently.

"Great, I'll be right down," said Marrio. He thanked the concierge, and she could only gaze into his dark-brown eyes. Marrio turned and headed out of the hotel.

CHAPTER SIXTEEN

Detectives Williams and Kaboo entered the precinct at about one thirty in the afternoon, right after a long lunch break. Kaboo still tasted bits of the grilled salmon and Jamaican spicy rice she had consumed along with a glass of sun tea. "That really hit the spot," she thought. "We ought to go to that place more often."

"You know that lunch was excellent and that the atmosphere was great," said Williams.

"Now that is strange, Wilson—I was just thinking something similar. We must be developing a telepathic link!" said Kaboo, laughing at the humor, appreciating that they could be on the same page without saying much at all. "Pretty soon, we'll be finishing each other's sentences."

"Hold on, Stella. That's what married people do, and you know I'm a die-hard bachelor," said Williams.

Kaboo thought he was a handsome man in his own rough and rugged way. Perhaps his strength and prudent, methodical mannerisms were what made him appealing. She had always felt chemistry between the two of them. She knew he felt it too, but neither of them had ever acted on the feeling—not only because of the professional character they each possessed and maintained, but also because they feared that romantic intimacy would destroy the great working relationship they had.

"Why couldn't life be simpler?" thought Kaboo.

She was indeed a pretty woman, about five feet nine in stature. She had a brown, beautiful complexion and hair that was short, curly, and dyed blond. If people had to guess what she did for a living, they would naturally assume that she was an Olympic track runner. She was proportioned perfectly, thanks to her strenuous workouts, which she did four times a week, and her running three miles every day. Williams looked at Kaboo at that instant, and she wondered whether they were having another telepathic moment.

After a slow second passed, Kaboo broke the moment and said, "Let's see what those surveillance tapes have for us. Out of the six we collected, maybe we'll get lucky." She reached into a file cabinet in their office, where they kept all items collected for their high-priority cases. These items included files, profiles, pictures, and surveillance tapes.

Kaboo put the first relevant surveillance tape into an electronic video projector, and she and Williams both viewed it together. Williams leaned over Kaboo's shoulder, drawing closer as if they were two droplets of rainwater that were drawing together to become one.

Kaboo felt her temperature rising. "Why don't we save some time; this may take a while, so why don't I look these over while you follow up with Antoinette Balestra's house sitter," she said.

Williams cleared his throat and nodded in accent, and then he went across the room to his desk and picked up the phone and began dialing.

Kaboo scanned the first tape and found nothing. The second tape revealed nothing as well. She placed the tape back in its bag and pulled out another. This one was from the jewelry store across the street from Jonell's Men's Wear. At first, nothing noticeable was found between 10:00 p.m. Tuesday night and 1:30 a.m. Wednesday morning, but then a tall black man and a shorter woman showed up on the tape; however, she knew that she and Williams could not identify the two people with any certainty because of the video's poor quality. Kaboo shouted, "Hey, Wilson, come here—I think I've found something."

Williams approached Kaboo and watched the screen as she played back the tape, stroking the whiskers on his chin. "Hmm, hard to make them out, but they look like our suspects. How far back did you rewind the tape?" he asked.

"Just to 10:00 p.m. I'll take it back further and see what we have." She started at 5:00 p.m. and ran the tape to 8:49 p.m.

"Well! Well! There you are! Nice, Stella, let's get this over to Detective Kwok; hopefully he can identify these two."

Stella called Detective Kwok, and his phone rang for a moment before he picked up. "Detective Le, Second Precinct," he said.

"Hey, Le. This is Stella. I'm faxing over some persons of interest; I need you to run them ASAP."

"No problem, Stella," he replied, and they both hung up.

CHAPTER SEVENTEEN

The morning sky was soft blue with shades of orange, vibrantly shining above the deeper-blue waters of the Caribbean. The sun had just risen, and the birds chirped busily in melodic, enthusiastic tones, while seagulls forged into the new day in search of food. Poised on the tall, tropical trees that bordered the hill, they waited like sentries and hunters, searching for signs of movement, scanning the sandy beach and the ocean's surface. A large, white seagull with a shiny, jet-black beak caught sight of a bluish-yellow fish, a blue tang, swimming playfully close to the surface. The large bird sprang from its branch and glided down speedily, claws wide open, eyes sharply on its prey, and it swiftly snatched the unsuspecting fish from the waters, carrying it back to the tree from which its quest began.

Not far from the water, a large, white house stood upon the rocky hillside, with its front facing the mighty body of water. A beautiful and young woman was standing on its porch and gazing at the new day. A voice called from inside the house: "Angelina, come in—breakfast is ready." It was Lucius Sucoy, her grandfather.

The young woman turned and headed inside, and a small dog followed her. Before she left the porch, she saw the moon fade and disappear, giving way to the morning sun. The large and white seagull, now at the base of the tree where it had started its hunt, was now feeding upon the once vibrant fish it had hoisted from the waters.

Ed rose a little earlier than usual and started his morning run late. Feeling the effects of a hangover from his long night at the club, he took off on his normal running path, thinking about his time at Xavier's. "That is some club. Kwame really has done well," he thought.

The club had an eloquent stage with a white, pearl-colored background. The shiny black floors were trimmed with gold, like his business card. The band had been great, but Ed was amazed at the dance floor, which was at the center of the club. The dance floor was essentially a clear top to a giant aquarium, through which ran giant water tubes that led to the VIP section and its tables, which were smaller fish tanks. Ed had never seen anything like that.

As Ed continued his run, he passed by the area of the homicide and thought back to the whole scenario. He gazed west and saw the moon as it gave way to the sun.

DETECTIVE WILLIAM'S CELL phone rang. He rolled over and took it from where it lay on the nightstand on the opposite side of his bed. "Detective Williams," he answered.

"Williams, this is Klein. I wanted to call you later, but I thought it best to get this information to you as soon as possible."

"What is it?" asked Williams.

"After we talked, I thought about Dugan and a couple of incidents we had with him. About four weeks ago, I was at the Starbucks over by Embassy Boulevard. I saw Dugan talking with a woman. I didn't think much of it because I was rushing to a meeting. I remember that we had to get prepared for a meeting about Caribbean Oil and that all the major companies and invested countries would be there. At the International Caribbean Oil Council meeting the following week, I saw the same woman sitting with the Royal Dutch Shell group.

"I don't know why I didn't think of this sooner. We prohibit our contractors and employees from mingling with our competitors, because of the sensitive confidential information our people know and handle. That is, the prohibition is meant to keep sensitive data from being leaked out.

"So, I asked some of our associates who used to work with Royal Dutch Shell, and this is what I found out: the woman is one of Royal Dutch Shell's executives, and she lives in the St. Donte Park area. You did say that Dugan's body was found in the park, right?"

"That's right," said Williams. "Did you happen to get her name? Would you recognize her again if you saw her?"

Klein paused, thinking. "Her name is Antoinette something; I think she is French. I am certain her first name is Antoinette—I remember it because one of my cousins shares the same first name—and, yes, I would recognize her."

"How about I swing by your office on Monday with some pictures to help you identify her. That work for you?" asked Williams.

"Any time after ten in the morning will be fine, Detective. I have an important engineer meeting before then, but I should be finished by that time," said Klein.

"Okay, I'll see you a little after ten," said Williams.

CHAPTER EIGHTEEN

Ed drove to the embassy and met Hernandez at the front door. "Good morning, sir," she said, saluting him.

"Good morning, soldier. Don't bother with the formalities from here on out. No need to salute every day—we're in this for the long haul. Now, what's our ambassador doing?" Ed asked.

"He's been in his office since seven this morning, been on the phone most of the time."

"Where is Thornton? And what time did you both get here?"

"Thornton is making rounds outside, and Ambassador Ballantyne was up and moving at 6:00 a.m."

"So we have an early riser. Did you and Thornton take turns and get rest last night?"

"Yes, sir, we did. We are both fresh, ready, and able."

"Great. Carry on, soldier."

ED'S PHONE RANG; the civilian Dennis Rollins, the team's computer geek, was calling. Ed answered the call. "Ed here."

"Sergeant Miller, sir, this is Rollins. I did the research you asked me to do, and I discovered some interesting coincidences. That dead man you found in the park two weeks ago happened to have ties with Ambassador Ballantyne. His name was Dugan Metcalf, and he was an engineer for oil-digging technology. He had several meetings with the ambassador right before he was taken out. And it seems that Royal Dutch Shell gained advantage toward securing the St. Vincent deep-dig rights shortly afterward."

"Okay, Rollins, make sure all the computers and communications in this building are secure, and make sure that whatever other information you gather is sent to me directly—and only me. From here on out, only call me on secured lines, and do the same with the others on our team."

It was a heck of a coincidence that Ed should stumble across a corpse that was somehow involved with Ambassador Ballantyne.

His phone rang again; this time it was Detective Williams. "Hello, Detective. What can I do for you?"

"Hello, Mr. Miller. I have information stating that you're involved with Ambassador Ballantyne—is that correct?"

"Yes, I'm in charge of his security detail. I'm here on official military business."

Williams thought for a second, remembering that Detective Le Kwok discovered that Dugan was on the surveillance footage at the embassy and was seen talking to the ambassador. Williams wondered whether Miller could possibly be involved in the murder. "Could you come down to the precinct, Mr. Miller? I'd like to ask you a few more questions."

"Sure, happy to oblige, Detective. Give me an hour, and I'll be there."

"See you then," said Williams.

Later, Ed entered the precinct and met Detective Le Kwok.

"What can I help you with?" asked Kwok.

"I'm looking for Detective Williams. He's expecting me" Ed said.

"Please, have a seat while I get him."

Williams, however, poked his head out to the main lobby and signaled Miller to follow him to his office. "I won't keep you long, Mr. Miller; I just have a few questions to ask you."

Kaboo, who was sitting at her desk across the room, got up and walked over and greeted Miller.

Williams started his questioning. "So, Mr. Miller, you say you are in charge of security for Ambassador Ballantyne."

"Yes, Detective, that's right. I don't know if there's much I can help you with, though—my work is confidential government business."

"Ah, I understand, Mr. Miller. Perhaps there is a rank I should use to address you?"

"I'm a sergeant," said Ed.

Williams nodded. "Sergeant Miller, did you know Dugan Metcalf?" he asked. Both detectives focused on the sergeant's body language when the question was asked. Kaboo wondered where Williams was going with this line of questioning.

"No, I didn't know him. My stumbling across his body was the first time I ever saw the man."

"He knew Ambassador Ballantyne. We have video footage of Dugan and Ballantyne meeting. Williams turned his computer around so Ed could see the clip of Ambassador Sydney and Dugan, meeting outside the Embassy doors, Ed noticed the Ambassadors aide Clarence Dupont, was also with them and Dugan was holding a briefcase. Williams continued his questioning. Did you know the ambassador is in the middle of a bidding war? For control of the oil rights, primarily between Mobile and Royal Dutch Shell? Oh, there are a few other players, and they all seem to be very aggressive toward getting those rights," said Williams.

Ed looked Williams in the eyes and glanced at Kaboo; though they tried to appear calm and relaxed, Ed could tell that they were intensely focused as they waited for his answer. Ed wondered what their pretext was, whether Williams was trying to pull his strings. He played along: "I can't speak on that, Detective, but what do I have to do with this?"

"Well, Sergeant, it is odd that you should be the one to stumble across Dugan's body. The US government is backing Mobile in this tug-of-war, and Metcalf just happened to be on the suspect table with Mobile, in regard to some delicate information concerning the rights to oil digging, which now seem to be in Royal Dutch Shell's favor. Metcalf was being investigated for espionage with Mobile, and he's been seen with Royal Dutch Shell's contacts and the ambassador. You want to know what it has to do with you? Right now, Sergeant Miller, you are a person of interest."

Williams was fishing, nothing more. "You're joking, right?" said Ed. "If you have any more questions for me about this, you will have to go through military procedures for civilian legal matters. You'll need to contact Captain Lemore of the US Army from here on out. Am I free to go?" Ed asked.

"Just one more thing, Sergeant. Do you know the ambassador's connection with Dugan?"

Ed shrugged, nothing more.

Williams grunted. "You're free to go."

Ed left the office, and Kaboo asked Williams, "What was that about? Are you now thinking this guy is involved in this murder?"

"What I'm thinking is our sergeant will start digging around on his side, and maybe something will surface that we can use," said Williams. He went over to the investigation board and pinned a picture of the sergeant next to those of the ambassador and the two-unidentified people from the park.

CHAPTER NINETEEN

Sydney Ballantyne looked in the bedroom of his two fifteen-year-old daughters, Shantel and Romara. Both girls were asleep, and Ballantyne thought of their mother, Alicia Benoit. She had passed away several years ago, in a freak car accident. He thought of the first time he saw her, when he was a student at St. George's University in Grenada. He met her at a soccer game on campus and tried several times to win her over, but she was very persistent on keeping her independence. She alone would decide how and when she was to be won. Sydney had not been the only one after her heart; there was Romeg Thomas also, a bright and promising mind, a young man with great potential, who studied political science. He was the son of a very successful and powerful man in St. Vincent. Sydney, however, was attending college on grants; he had come from meager beginnings but had great ambition and a large appetite for life.

Throughout the course of the year, both men pursued her, and their love triangle quickly climaxed. How cunningly she toyed with their affections as they pursued her heart. She delighted in their aggressive courting. Oh, how much Sydney had wanted to win her over. Back then, he was not the powerful and influential man that he would become.

Sydney, reflecting on his memories of when they were at the Cotillion Ball, remembered his asking her to dance that night, which she did. However, she was still being courted aggressively by Romeg. Sydney reflected on that night of the Cotillion Ball. That night, his cocky adversary challenged him to a fight for her, to once and for all sever Sydney's connection to Alicia. Romeg egged young Ballantyne on, using condescending words to insult Sydney's place and class in life. He did this in front of Alicia and their peers, demeaning and belittling him relentlessly. Sydney, however, was sharp and witty with his rebuttals, keeping pace comment for comment. Romeg might have won the battle if he had not doubled down and made one fatal mistake: he challenged Sydney to an old-fashioned fistfight, hoping to prove that he was more masculine than young Ballantyne, hoping to convince Alicia of his physical superiority.

Sydney was no stranger to the art of fighting. He was in the Grenadine Boxing Club, even sponsored by a person in the alumni who had seen potential in young Ballantyne and had chosen to support him throughout his college years. Romeg was bigger than Ballantyne and was an athlete playing on the college's soccer team, but he was not a match for Sydney's fighting skills.

Romeg attacked Sydney quickly, throwing a right hook. Sydney ducked, and the blow merely brushed against his shoulder. Romeg continued with another attempt—this time a left roundhouse punch, which Sydney blocked with his right hand. Sydney countered the assault by rapidly pummeling Romeg with both fists. The fight ended before it ever really began.

Sydney looked down over his victim and then at Alicia, whose eyes were wide open with excitement from the intensity and glory of the battle for her hand. Romeg had been humiliated in front of friends, family, and the woman he had hoped to win.

This all happened during the romantic and prominent Cotillion Ball, and Sydney realized that he had finally won the affection of Alicia, the woman he loved. His victory, however, came with a price: along with winning Alicia's favor, he also gained an enemy for life. Romeg Thomas vowed that he would get back at Sydney.

"One day, my dear Sydney—yes, one day," he said, before quitting the scene to nurse his bruised body and ego.

Sydney's mind wandered back to the present.

Morning was in full bloom, and the girls were rising for school. Yolanda Hernandez was there to escort them. "Good morning, Ambassador. I'm here to take the girls to school," she said. She was wearing brown jeans, a blue denim shirt, and a tan jacket, which concealed her 9 mm Berretta.

The twins could be told apart because Romara had a noticeable scar on her right hand, which she got from playing tennis and chasing after a low ball; she had slid on the ground and scraped the back of her hand, cutting it deep on the ragged edge of the cement. She was tough and scrappy like her dad, and Shantel was more like her mom, the princess type, though she had a bit of mischief about her. The girls came into the kitchen, where the ambassador and Hernandez were waiting.

"This is Ms. Yolanda," said Sydney, "and she is going to be escorting you during the time we are here. I want you to be nice and listen to her. I expect you to be on your best behavior."

"Hello, girls. How you doin'?" said Hernandez.

Neither of the girls answered. The ambassador quickly chastised them: "You will display good manners and properly address Ms. Hernandez whenever she speaks to you."

The girls then apologized and offered their good mornings.

Hernandez, after accepting their apologies with equal good manners, said, "Okay, I'll be right here in the other room, waiting for you girls to get ready to go. There will be plenty of time to get to know each other."

The girls wolfed down their breakfasts, remembering that they needed to get to school quickly: they had a big day ahead of them because their basketball team was currently in first place, and there was a buzz of excitement going around the school, which the girls wanted to bask in. They grabbed their bags and rushed past Yolanda to the car waiting outside. Hernandez followed right behind them.

CHAPTER TWENTY

Williams went to his desk, picked up his dinosaur of a push-button phone, and dialed the number of Balestra's house sitter. The old black AT&T phone had belonged to his father, who had been a detective before him, as had been Williams's grandfather. Williams kept the phone as a sentimental piece, a reminder of his family's legacy. He heard the phone ringing, and a woman answered.

Williams said, "Hello, is Beverly there?

"Yes, this is she."

"This is Detective Williams from the Second Precinct. I would like to ask you a few questions about an incident that occurred during your house sitting at Antoinette Balestra's house. Can you meet with me today?"

"Who did you say you were?" asked Beverly.

"Detective Williams at the Second Precinct. I handle homicides."

"Okay, I can meet you, but where?"

"I will come to your place. We have your address. I will see you in, let's say, thirty minutes. Is that okay?"

"Okay," said Beverly.

Detective Williams grabbed his notepad and the keys to his brown Impala SS and headed out to see Beverly. He went without Kaboo, because she and Le Kwok were still trying to identify the two murder suspects.

Williams arrived at Beverly's neighborhood after a twenty-minute drive. She lived in a safe, working-class neighborhood; the homes were moderate and well maintained. The only chaos Williams noticed was a dog running loose in the streets. The people looked friendly and active. Overall, the community gave Williams a pleasant impression. After he reached her home, he parked his car and took ten minutes to go over some notes. He then got out and went to her front door and rang the bell. A young woman answered.

"Hi, I'm looking for Beverly," said Williams.

"Yes, I'm Beverly."

"I'm Detective Williams. May I come in?" he asked after showing her his badge.

"Sure, Detective, come in. How can I help you?"

"I understand that you did some house sitting for Antoinette Balestra on a Tuesday night two weeks ago. Is that right?"

"Yes, I did."

"On that night, there was a murder behind Balestra's home. Do you remember anything about that evening?"

Beverly took a moment to think. "I didn't know about the murder until Ms. Balestra mentioned it to me on Monday, about a week ago. When we spoke, I remembered that I had not told her about the person that had knocked on the door that night. When I told her about the person, she was surprised."

"You said a man came to the door. Do you have any idea who he was?" asked Williams.

"No, I didn't answer the door. Ms. Balestra gave me firm instructions not to answer the door or her telephone. She said that if she needed to contact me, she would call my cell phone."

"I see," said Williams. "Did she say why she didn't want you to answer the door or telephone?"

"She just wanted me to feel safe about being alone in her home."

Williams sighed. "It's too bad you didn't see what he looked like."

"Oh! I did see him! I looked through the peephole. He was a white man with a lot of blond hair. Yes, I remember that he had a black briefcase and that he seemed nervous. He was creepy. I went upstairs and peeped out one of the front bedroom windows, where I had been watching TV, and watched him leave. He actually went around to the side of the house."

"You mean toward the walkway to Saint Donte Park?" asked Williams.

"Yes!"

"Did you describe the man to Ms. Balestra?"

"No, it didn't seem important at the time, and Ms. Balestra had other things on her mind."

"And what time did the man knock?"

"Oh, about eleven thirty. I know because I had dozed off while watching the *Late Show*, and I remember checking the time on my cell phone before I went to look through the peephole."

"And you said you didn't know or see anything the next morning. There was quite a bit of noise behind the house when the police arrived in the park."

"I have an early day job, and I had to pull a double shift that Wednesday, so I left the house about four thirty that morning."

"Ah, I see," said Williams. "So you couldn't have been aware of the incident."

"That's right, Detective!"

"And was that the first time you talked with Ms. Balestra since you watched her house that week ago?" asked Williams.

Beverly seemed a little nervous at that point, sensing that the detective was asking too many questions about Ms. Balestra. "I don't think I can help you anymore, Detective. Please, I have errands to run," she said.

"Thank you for your time, Beverly—you've been very helpful. Oh, I have one more question: when did you expect Ms. Balestra to return from her trip?"

"She was supposed to come back Wednesday, but she texted me saying she would not get back until Thursday and not to worry about watching the house Wednesday night. Is that all, Detective?"

"Yes, thank you, Beverly."

"Good-bye."

Detective Williams left the house and got into his Impala SS. He called Kaboo. "Hey, Stella. I've got some interesting information: it looks like Dugan Metcalf was paying Ms. Balestra a visit the night of the murder. I have a funny feeling she doesn't know it was Dugan's body that we found in the park behind her home."

"It's a good thing we never released his name on the news. Time to visit Ms. Balestra again," said Kaboo.

"Yeah, it's that time—let's see what she really knows. I'll be back at the office in twenty minutes. See you then."

CHAPTER TWENTY-ONE

Detective Le Kwok had researched the two murder suspects and found out they were not Americans or from St. Vincent. They were Portuguese. The black man had a rap sheet, but Bastalayo police would have to go through the Caribbean International Police Co-op for jurisdiction and to get the relevant intel. Doing so would take time not only because all the political dots were not yet in place but also because the explosion of oil exploration had illuminated the faults in the region's interconnected legal systems.

The white woman had not yet appeared in any computer files, which might mean that she was undercover or an assassin for hire or had not yet been caught or involved in any investigations. Kwok wondered about whom she could be connected to.

To speed up his search, Kwok gave the man's description to his department's FBI contact, hoping to cut through the red tape to identify the guy more quickly. The FBI contact said, "Give me twenty-four hours, and I'll see what I can find out."

ED AND MARRIO were driving to the Embassy. Ed had called ahead to Randell Thornton to check out how the weekend went. Thornton replied that everything had gone well. Yolanda Hernandez was with the girls at their private school, and Dennis Rollins was on site at the embassy, tweaking surveillance instruments and continually scanning the air waves for anything unusual.

The ambassador was in his office, bogged down with a stack of documents. When Ed and Marrio walked in the embassy, the ambassador's assistant approached them. "Sergeant Miller, the ambassador would like to see you right away," he said.

Ed knocked on the ambassador's office door and then walked in, Marrio following him.

"Sergeants Miller and Sanchez, good morning to the both of you. I want to go over my agenda for today. I will be meeting with Royal Dutch Shell, so I have to go to the Sheraton Hotel on Castillo Street at 12:00 p.m. I have one more appointment with my girls; they have a musical performance at a party today at 4:00 p.m. We will be going to the home of a prominent business associate of mine, so I need your people to be low-key. I don't want my associates to catch wind there is a problem. So how will you plan to do all this?"

Ed's plan was to give Thornton the day off, seeing that he and Hernandez had covered the weekend for forty-eight hours straight. "Today, Sergeant Sanchez and I will stay with you. Hernandez will keep watch over the girls, and she can dress the part to fit into your event. I'll have Rollins, my tech man, track us by using the surveillance cameras on the vehicle—cameras that can point and scan all directions. We also will dress to blend in; this is not our first rodeo, Ambassador. Sergeant Marrio and I will have hidden-eye camera gear, so we won't look conspicuous. Rollins will be our eyes. It will all go smoothly."

"Okay, Sergeant," said the ambassador.

Marrio's phone rang. He excused himself to answer the call. "Hello," he said.

"Sergeant Sanchez, sir, this is Private Buchanan at supplies. Your special order is ready."

"Have all of my requirements been met?"

"Yes, sir."

"Great," said Marrio, "I'm on my way. Thank you, Private." Marrio ended the call and updated Ed, and then he left Sydney's office.

Ed was busy wondering what connection the ambassador could possibly have with Dugan Metcalf, but he decided to hold off on such questions for now, to simply observe things for a while and let something surface. "Ambassador," he said, "I need to go over a few things with my men before we take off. I'll leave you to your work."

Later that morning, Marrio reached the government supply center at about eight thirty. "Hello, I'm Sergeant Marrio Sanchez, and I have a delivery to pick up." He showed his identification to Private Buchanan, the same soldier who had called him. The soldier was at the loading dock with Marrio's special order.

"Everything in order, Private?" asked Marrio.

"It appears so, sir. Here are your keys."

The private handed Marrio the keys to a jet-black Lincoln Continental, which had been shipped in from the states for this assignment. The car was custom designed. It was bulletproof, and it had special built-in weaponry for offense and defense. Cameras with night vision and heat sensors could watch every direction. It had concealed machine guns in its front and rear ends and could travel on water. Marrio and Ed were familiar with these vehicles; they had used them in the Sudan during the genocide war. Marrio and Ed guarded American diplomats and UN peacekeepers during that time. "What a hell of a situation," thought Marrio, thinking back on the experience. He pushed the memories away from his mind.

"Okay, looks good. Thank you, Private," said Marrio.

"You're welcome, sir."

Marrio left the supply building and returned to the embassy a little after nine thirty later that morning.

Everything went as planned, and eleven o'clock rolled around. The ambassador wrapped up his morning work and carefully put away the documents he had been working on. Ed and the ambassador walked out to the new Lincoln, and the ambassador was impressed. "I don't believe I've seen a car like this before," he said.

"Yeah," said Ed, "it's not your grandfather's Buick—that's for sure."

"What do you mean?"

"Oh, it's an American expression, just means that things have changed. New generation, new toys."

"Oh, I see."

"After you, Ambassador," said Ed.

The ambassador got into the plush car, and Ed followed him after looking around and scoping out the area. Marrio stayed behind the wheel while Ed kept in contact with Rollins. "How's the view, Rollins?" he said.

"Clear on all sides, sir."

"Okay, let's roll."

CHAPTER TWENTY-TWO

Day Sixteen: Reflections

E d looked over the interior of the car, and thoughts of Sudan came back to him. He thought back to the mission he was sent on there, during the time of Sudan's bloody revolution, and it was certainly no place to be. He was part of a team assigned to protect Americans, dignitaries, and peacekeepers, who had been sent there to assess the severity of the war and then report back to their hierarchy. The Sudan revolution was one of the world's biggest political issues of its time, an issue in which the United States played a major role in the peacekeeping efforts. Ed had made some assessments himself after witnessing the violent scenes, wondering how people could create so much death, could take the lives of so many men, women, and children. Most of the children had become war orphans. War did not discriminate; it was a glutton that never felt satiated, always devouring as much life as people were willing to give. In regard to power, no one ever gave it up willingly—it had to be taken. Ed had seen power grabs paid for by human lives, and they always made him sick. It was a sight he never would get used to.

He remembered thanking God, knowing that what happened in Sudan could have happened to his country, his people, and his family. "There go I, except by the grace of God," he thought. He was a soldier and wise in a worldly manner, but he knew his creator, and his creator knew him.

He remembered one day. He had been counting his blessings when he heard a loud boom. About two hundred yards away from where he and his unit were standing, a car bomb had gone off. The two people in the car were immediately killed, and several people in close vicinity were injured. People were running everywhere in wild pandemonium and fearing for their lives. Ed quickly went into action, yelling for his unit to get the dignitaries into a nearby building, pushing a male dignitary so hard that he almost fell to the ground. His unit took cover and immediately set up a perimeter around the building, scanning the area. He shouted quick orders to his men, telling all of them to draw their weapons and prepare to fire. After the last of the dignitaries were rushed inside their improvised shelter, Ed immediately established communications with his commanding officers and gave a quick assessment, also known as an ACE report, for his unit's ammo, casualties, and equipment.

He spoke with Steven Kurtzberg, the man at the top of the chain of command, and they coordinated air support to extract the casualties and dignitaries; meanwhile, Ed's unit hastily set up defensive positions and prepared to return fire. The most difficult part soon came: he and his unit would have to expose their position to set up a hot landing zone, in which the helicopters could safely come in to evacuate the casualties and dignitaries.

Ed called to Marrio, who grabbed a smoke grenade and tossed it on the spot where the helicopter could land. The members of their unit repositioned themselves by thinning the lines and falling back to the extraction point, where they provided overwatch protection until the extraction was completed. But hostiles appeared with fully automatic rifles, and they entrenched themselves behind a four-foot wall about six hundred feet from the landing zone. Ed knew that his unit could not extract the civilians with those enemies present—they would mow down the civilians in a matter of seconds if they had the chance. Ed knew those hostiles had to be taken out before anyone could be evacuated.

Ed crawled across the ground to a Lincoln Sedan, one of his unit's bulletproof vehicles; staying low, he managed to climb in unnoticed. Once inside, he fired her up and threw her into gear, spinning the car around in the direction of the wall. The hostiles sprayed the front of the Lincoln with bullets but were not able to penetrate the bulletproof glass. Ed opened the center compartment and pulled on the red latch inside, engaging the loaded heavy-caliber machine guns on the front of the car, which spit out round after round, melting the wall into a pile of rubble, killing every hostile that had been hiding behind it.

Marrio led the dignitaries out while Ed remained behind the guns. The members of Ed's unit were the last Americans to leave, making sure that all personnel had been safely extracted. Gunships circling above the compound provided air support for Ed and his men and escorted them to a designated rally point, where they were eventually extracted.

"*That* car had not been built for grandpa," thought Ed, coming out of his memories.

CHAPTER TWENTY-THREE

E d and his team were driving down the busy boulevard. As the afternoon approached, the lunch crowd was out along the streets, congesting the traffic. Marrio was behind the wheel and was concerned because the traffic had come close to a standstill. Looking up ahead, he could see commotion. The intersection was blocked by what looked like an accident.

"We've got a situation," said Marrio through his radio.

"I see," said Ed. "What does it look like up ahead?"

"We are at a standstill. Looks like a fender bender up ahead. We need to take a detour."

Ed and Marrio were on high alert, each suspecting that the traffic jam was more than an accident. Meanwhile, Ambassador Ballantyne was going over last-minute details for his meeting with Royal Dutch Shell.

Marrio said, "There's an alley up ahead, about one hundred feet away, and on my right. I could take it."

Ed called Rollins to get a surveillance report: "What do you see, Rollins?"

Rollins responded immediately: "I'm picking up body heat on the top of the roof to your left, about two hundred feet ahead. Doesn't look good, sir. I'm detecting weapons as well."

"Hit it, Marrio—we're in an ambush," said Ed.

"I'm on it, sir."

Marrio veered right and jumped the car onto the sidewalk. Two ladies holding lattes and lunch bags scrambled out of the way, shouting obscenities as the car whizzed by. Three pings sharply struck the passenger-side glass on the back-left side of the vehicle. A man standing just a few feet away from the car was hit by one of the rebounding bullets and went down.

"We're under fire," said Marrio.

"No kidding, man," said Ed. "Rollins, can you find the shooters on your cameras?"

"I'm zooming in now, sir. Looks like two white males. One is using a sniper rifle; the other is holding binoculars."

"What's up ahead in that alley?" asked Ed.

"Looks clear, sir. I have pics on that auto accident too."

"Okay, keep tracking the sniper and spotter on the rooftop, and don't let them get away."

Rollins switched over to satellite surveillance to watch the shooters. They took off and entered the building.

Marrio said, "I need a new route—we got heavy traffic up ahead."

"Rollins, I need you to find us a way out of here," said Ed. "Switch communications to Marrio."

Rollins put the surveillance cameras on automatic tracking to keep beads on the shooters and then connected another set of the Lincoln's cameras to satellite signals and GPS. "Two blocks up ahead, sir, we've got a clear street that leads to a small bridge. That bridge will take you into a residential neighborhood filled with single-story homes—that is, there aren't many tall buildings in that neighborhood."

"Scan the area for more shooters," said Marrio.

"Ambassador," said Ed, "we're going to have to cancel your meeting."

"No way, soldier—I didn't get where I am today by running scared," said the ambassador.

"Someone just tried to kill you. We just need to evaluate the situation before you move forward."

Sydney was a stubborn man, and not much frightened him. He simply snorted, once.

"Hernandez," said Ed, "we're under attack. This is a red alert, so grab the girls and go to the heightened security plan. Get Thornton ASAP for backup. I'll fill you in later."

"Yes, sir," said Yolanda.

"I lost the shooters," said Rollins. "They are either in the building or had an underground escape route."

"Okay, Rollins, we'll get back to them later," said Ed.

"I will not miss this meeting," said Sydney. "My country is counting on me. Soldier, do you risk life and limb for your country?"

Ed thought about what the ambassador said. "Without a doubt, sir."

"Then you must understand what I must do."

"Okay, but I'll have to run full surveillance of the meeting place first, and we must alert Royal Dutch Shell to have maximum security on hand now—or the meeting is off."

The ambassador simply nodded and called his Royal Dutch Shell contacts and passed on Ed's prerequisites for the meeting.

Marrio worked with Rollins to pursue a safe escape route. After they cleared the bridge, Rollins had Marrio veer right and head up a small residential street with dense trees. At the end of the street, there was a strip mall and a wholesale store for food; both places were fairly busy. As Marrio passed the first driveway, a van darted out with a machine gun pointed out of its passenger-side window. The gun fired several bursts at the rear glass of the Lincoln.

Marrio made a hard right onto a driveway that led to the strip mall and drove to the back of the lot, moving away from the congested part of the parking lot. People scrambled and screamed as both vehicles barreled down the lane. Marrio made another sharp turn, and Ed rolled halfway out of the car, holding his 9 mm Smith & Wesson. As the van made the turn, Ed fired, putting two bullets in the chest and one in the head of the shooter.

Marrio slammed on the breaks, forcing the van to rear-end the Lincoln. He jumped out of the driver's seat. Before the other driver could recover from the jolt of the crash, Marrio used his 9 mm to execute him.

Ed came up from behind, checking the rear seats, making sure both men were neutralized. The men were dead. Marrio and Ed jumped back into the Lincoln and sped off.

Ed pulled out Detective Williams's card and called his number.

"This is Detective Williams."

"This is Sergeant Miller. Detective, we have just been assaulted and had to take out two assailants in the Romy Shopping Plaza, south of the Layton Bridge. I have the ambassador with me. It was self-defense, and I'm giving you a heads-up."

"What! Where are you now?" asked Williams.

"I can't tell you that, Detective. I'll get back with you after we get the ambassador to safety."

Ed hung up, and Detective Williams called the police dispatch. "Get all patrol cars in the area to the Romy Shopping Plaza on the double. There has been a shootout. Two men are possibly dead in a car, but assume that they are alive, armed, and dangerous—proceed with heavy caution."

"Detective Williams, we have reports of a black Lincoln fleeing the area."

"Okay, tell our people about the black Lincoln. Do not stop it or engage. Follow it from a safe distance."

As the team's Lincoln vacated the area, Ed inspected the pings on the glass. He looked at the ambassador, who was still calm. Ed respected the tough, gritty heart of the ambassador and admired him for his courage. Men with such fortitude were rare.

The ambassador looked at Ed, knowing what Ed had to tell him: "We will not be attending today's meeting, after all."

CHAPTER TWENTY-FOUR

Thornton and Ed took the night watch over the ambassador's home. Rollins enhanced the surveillance equipment, and Ed had bulletproof glass petitions brought in to cover every window in the ambassador's home. Marrio and Hernandez rested through the night, knowing that they would cover Tuesday night.

Marrio rose fairly early Tuesday morning and went for his normal six-mile run. He decided to have his Harley shipped to the island, figuring that if he was going to be there for six months, then he needed his wheels. After finishing his run, he entered the lobby of the Buerada Hotel and ran into Crystal LeBlanc. It was almost nine thirty, and she was about to take a break.

"Good morning," said Marrio.

"Good morning," said Crystal. "Oh my, you're a sweaty mess."

"Yeah, that's what happens after six miles of running."

Crystal walked from the reservation desk toward the hotel's café. Marrio could smell the freshly brewed coffee and decided to get some too.

"Hey, Crystal, I'm going to get a cup of coffee. May I buy you one?"

"I was just about to do that myself."

They walked side by side to the café.

"Try not to get any of your sweatiness on me," said Crystal.

"No worries."

In the café, a thin young man stood behind the counter and waited for Marrio's order.

"I'll have a large black coffee, no sugar, and whatever the lady wants."

"A small latte, please," said Crystal.

They sat at a corner table in the cafe. The room was quite quaint, offering books, hats, shirts, assorted souvenirs, and figurines. Each corner of the café had a large, tropical plant, each the size of a small tree, and soft jazz could be heard in the background. Marrio looked over to the stand closest to him and saw a carving; it was a woman dancing barefoot on sand while a man appeared frozen in awe at her presence. The tide rippled up the sand, and the moon was full in the backdrop.

"So I guess Mr. Miller assigned you to have coffee with me, seeing that he hasn't gotten around to it himself."

Marrio laughed. "No, I forgot he had plans to have coffee with you, but no worries, I'm better company."

"Oh, are you? Why is that?"

"You know I'd tell you, but I would rather show you."

"And what will you show me?"

"I'm having my motorcycle shipped here to the island. Why don't you let me take you for a ride? You can show me the island, and I can show you adventure."

Crystal gazed at Marrio, sensing that he was more than the common man, and she enjoyed the mystery he expressed through his words and motions. And being taken in by a sense of intrigue, she said, "Okay, yes, you get your bike, and I will take you up on that ride. And what about your buddy, Mr. Miller?"

"No worries. We live by the motto All's Fair in Love and War."

"Oh! So that's what this is?" asked Crystal.

Marrio laughed and then gazed again at the figurine, not quite sure why it grabbed his attention.

THE DAY APPEARED calm and quiet. The Ambassador and his daughters went about their normal routine, although the team was on high alert, everyone was able to relax for the moment. Ed doubted anyone would try another attempt on the ambassador's life anytime soon.

Standing in one of the back offices at the embassy, he could smell the fresh pot of coffee, that Rollins had made. Walking to the kitchen, he picked a green and white coffee mug from the dish cabinet, that displayed the flag of St. Vincent. Grabbing the pot of coffee, he filled the cup, leaving it black with no sugar, then sipped it. "Man, he sure has this coffee making down pat" speaking to himself in a low tone. Rollins was a coffee connoisseur. No one knew what was in it, just that he brewed his coffee slow, and it was right up there with the best they had ever tasted. It had become one of those little things the team looked forward to each day. After a few more sips, Ed went over in his mind, what had transpired since the attack on the Ambassador. Detective Williams came up in his thinking. Just then, the cell phone rang.

"Sergeant, this is Detective Williams. I need to see you today."

"I figured," said Ed. "We will be down to your precinct, and you should expect to get a call from army intelligence in the near future."

"We already have. I just need to establish a few ground rules here."

"No problem, Detective."

"Call me Wilson."

"Okay, Wilson. Call me Ed."

The rest of the week passed, and all remained quiet.

CHAPTER TWENTY-FIVE

Week Four: Sunday

Marrio's phone rang. It was Hernandez.

"Sergeant Sanchez, sir."

"What is it Hernandez?"

"Checking in, sir. I'm on duty with you tonight. What time should we meet up?"

"Meet me at 4:00 p.m. at the air force base's gym, and bring your workout gear."

"Will we be working out, sir?"

"Something like that, Hernandez. Don't be late."

Having already tested Thorntons weapon skills, Marrio wanted to test Hernandez's fighting skills and see if she was as good as she claimed to be. He needed to know for himself what he was working with.

"Yes, sir," said Hernandez.

Later, she arrived at the gym fifteen minutes early. Marrio was already in the boxing ring and geared up in gloves and headgear.

Marrio said, "Gear up and get in the ring, Hernandez. There are gloves and headgear over there."

"Are you serious, sir?" asked Hernandez.

"Doesn't it look like I'm serious, soldier? Are you going to question me or get in here and show me what you got?"

She walked over to the gear Marrio had put out for her and put it on. Wanting to kid around, she threw a snide question out to the sergeant: "Is this like a rivalry thing between a Puerto Rican and a Mexican?"

Marrio laughed. "You got jokes, Hernandez. Look, I'm going to take it easy on you, seeing as you're the weaker gender."

"Don't do me any favors, sir. I don't want to hear any excuses after I kick your butt."

"Well, you're cocky enough now—I hope you bring that grit into the ring. I'll give you five minutes to warm up."

Hernandez slid through the ropes and did a few stretches and continued her trash talking. Marrio regarded her coolness and the confidence in her voice and was pleased with her character. He was hoping that she would be just as good as she had claimed. "Are you ready yet?" he asked.

"Let's rock, sir."

They circled each other within the ring, feeling one another out. Marrio stood in a boxing stance; Hernandez, a karate stance.

"Any special style, sir?" asked Hernandez.

"No, just give me what you got. And call me Sarge."

Yolanda started with several jabs to get a feel for the distance. Marrio blocked each one. He then threw a few of his own. Hernandez countered with a roundhouse right and a left-hand uppercut, almost catching Marrio.

"Not bad," said Marrio. "Show me something else."

Hernandez faked a right and forward kick and then swept it around to her left. Again, Marrio blocked it, retaliating with a half-effort left hook, which glanced Hernandez's shoulder as she swerved out of the way.

"Don't hold back, Sarge—I thought you were a bad boy," said Hernandez.

Marrio lunged forward with a left and right combo, followed with a straight kick, pounding Hernandez back into the ropes."

"Is that what you mean, Hernandez?" asked Marrio.

Hernandez frowned, giving him a look, and then put her head down and lunged forward, this time throwing two left jabs, a right hook, and a left uppercut, and then swinging around with a reverse punch. The last blow caught Marrio on the jaw.

Marrio fell back a few steps and shook his head. He looked at Hernandez and smiled, nodding to her in approval. "Nice move. You put together a sweet combination. You think you can do that again?"

Hernandez waited for Marrio to start his attack. He opened with a left kick to the side of the head and then a right roundhouse to the body. Hernandez blocked both shots. She then faked a left kick and followed with a right kick, which Marrio smothered with his arms, twisting her leg and slamming Hernandez to the mat on her back. Bending over her as if to gloat at besting her, he looked down at her, squinting with one eye as if to say, "That's it?"

Just then, Hernandez thrust the front of her left foot between Marrio's legs, aiming for the man zone. Marrio caught the move just in time, keeping the blow from having full impact, but it still had enough momentum to put the fear of Jesus in him.

"What the heck was that, Hernandez?" he asked.

"I never said I fought fair, Sarge—I fight to win."

"Well, I'm glad you're on my side. That's enough for today, soldier. Let's get out of here and get something to eat. You and I are on duty tonight."

CHAPTER TWENTY-SIX

Four weeks had passed, and the team moved out of the Buerada Hotel and settled in a house down the street from the ambassador. Fortunately, the house belonged to an ex–navy admiral, who was now a consultant for corporate businesses, and he lived primarily in San Diego. He had purchased the home as a getaway spot and used it only two months out of the year. The ambassador had pulled a few strings to get it.

The house was on the corner, and Rollins set up surveillance on the rooftop to cover the nearby streets. The ambassador's home was at the end of a cul-de-sac, so everything could be seen from the front. Rollins set up cameras and hi-tech body-heat detectors around the sides and back of the house, the detectors essentially pointing to any spots that an assailant or sniper might try to set up. Also, tiny motion detectors and hidden cameras were set on nearby trees and lampposts to catch pictures of suspicious people.

"Looks good so far," said Ed. "How much more do you have to set up?"

"That's it, sir," said Rollins. "We're good to go. Not even a fly can get in this area without me knowing it."

"That's what I like to hear. Can you show Thornton and Hernandez how to use your system?"

"No problem. I'll have them up to speed in no time."

Ed went over the operation with his team and laid out a daily plan. "Hernandez, you'll work with Marrio, and Thornton and I will pair up for the night watch. Two will stay in the house each night, and we will alternate our roles. Rollins, this is your HQ; Hernandez and Thornton will take over for you when you need a break. Okay, we all know the job—let's get to it. Marrio, you're on."

Marrio slapped Hernandez on the shoulder and said, "Let's go, soldier. We got work to do!"

"Yes, sir," said Hernandez, and they walked out toward the ambassador's house.

Rollins proceeded to teach Thornton about the surveillance setup.

"I'm going out for a run and to check out the area; I won't be long," said Ed.

After leaving the house, he headed west toward the beach, which was about two miles away. The rest of the houses in the area were widely spread apart. ATV and dirt-bike tracks ran through the sandy dirt, between and behind the homes, all along the paths. Various tropical trees and plants covered the landscape, sometimes densely, sometimes sparsely. Ed came across the main beach road, which he turned onto, heading to a park. Running at a strong pace and breathing heavily, he smelled the salt of the ocean and felt the cool of its breeze; it was intoxicating and made him run faster and harder. The people in the park observed him as a warrior, cheering him on as though he were in an Olympic race.

Meanwhile, off in the distance and on top of a hill overlooking the ocean park, there was a woman walking a small, white Terrier. She heard the commotion and turned to see where it was coming from.

CHAPTER TWENTY-SEVEN

"Okay, Shantel, Romara, let's go. You don't want to be late; this is not how successful people do things," said Sydney Ballantyne to his daughters. Marrio was watching the morning news on the living-room television. Hernandez did her morning security check, and Rollins helped her by scanning the neighborhood with his advanced camera system. Ambassador Ballantyne would work from home that day. Marrio figured it would be a quiet day, but he still observed everything around them with a keen eye, seeking to remain on high alert.

Hernandez left with the girls, taking them to school, and Thornton would trail them until the girls were safely on the school's premises. Hernandez would stay close to the school to watch over the girls, and Thornton would come back to base and continue learning about the surveillance system, with the help of Rollins.

Marrio thought about Crystal, and the date they were to have. He had talked to her several times but had been unable to see her because of the intense security routine he and his team were executing. His motorcycle had arrived, and he wanted more than ever to take it and her out for a spin. "I've got to call her now," he thought. "This Friday I'm off, so we can do it then." He did one more check of the house with Rollins to make sure everything was secure; then he called her.

"Hello, Crystal. This is Marrio."

"Hi, Marrio. How are you?"

"I'm great. How are you doing?"

"Fine, it's nice to hear from you."

"Yeah, it's nice to hear your voice. I sure miss seeing you and having coffee with you. I looked forward to those mornings."

"Yeah, me too. It was fun. So when will I see you? Are you going to remain this busy all the time you are here? If so, I won't get to see you."

Marrio lit up when he heard these words of assurance: her feelings were clearly on the same page as his. "It's a day-to-day thing, but I promise I'll make it happen; I'll find the time to get there. How about Friday? I have the day off, and I have my bike—it arrived this week. I want to take you on a ride."

"Really?—I'd love to go for a ride! I've been waiting for this. I work until five, so will the evening be okay?"

Marrio wanted the whole day, but if an evening was all she could offer, he would take it happily—having her all to himself for an evening would be a slice of paradise. Just Crystal, him, and Hell Fighter…sounded marvelous. "Ah, okay, how about seven o'clock?"

She heard a little discouragement in his tone but quickly realized that he wanted more. "I can take the day off. I'm sure I can get my assistant manager to switch days with me; then you and I can spend the whole day together. I just need to check some things in the morning. Can you be here at about nine thirty in the morning?"

Marrio's posture soared when he heard this. "Hell yeah!—I'm sorry, I mean yeah! That would be great. Let's do it."

"See you then, bye."

"Okay, bye."

He hung up feeling on cloud nine, clapped his hands together in a loud, exuberant fashion, and said, "Thank you, Lord."

Ambassador Ballantyne walked in on the tail end of the merriment and heard Marrio's exclamation of joy. He smiled and then continued to the kitchen for a glass of water. He thought, "It's good to see some happiness."

CHAPTER TWENTY-EIGHT

It was now four weeks into the Metcalf case, and things had come to a standstill.

Detective Le Kwok got a return call from the FBI connection, who had been unable to find information about the white woman involved in the murder. The trail toward identifying the two suspects had become quite cold. No local cameras around the entire area had picked up anything; the airport and the port authority knew nothing; and the police's local street snitches had no information either.

"I'm puzzled that no one has seen these suspects," said Williams. "Not a single local camera around the entire area has caught a glimpse of them. The airport and port authorities—nothing. Even our street snitches come up empty."

"Maybe the suspects had a private boat," said Kaboo.

"Maybe, but I checked that. We've got a lot of connections at the docks, so you'd think they would notice if a strange boat had docked and left; besides that, the Coast Guard works day and night monitoring these waters."

"Seems the suspects know how to stay under our radar. Hey, why don't we call it an early day and go get a drink? I'll buy."

"Are you trying to hit on me, Stella?"

"If I was a guy and told you let's get a drink, would you think I was hitting on you?" asked Kaboo.

Williams thought, "You are hardly a guy, and truth be told, it's hard enough being near you when we are at work."

"Well?" said Kaboo, snapping him out of his thoughts.

"I don't know, Stella—if you were a guy, you might roll like that."

"Really, Wilson, you need to stop clowning."

"All right, Stella, let's get that drink. I'll call Kwok and have him cover for us."

Soon, Williams and Kaboo were driving to a small but well-known tavern on the eastern side of the island. It took about thirty minutes to drive there. They arrived right when happy hour was starting, a little after four o'clock. Williams ordered Crown Royal on the rocks; Kaboo, a chocolate Sex Panther.

"Let's say we turn these radios down for now, Stella," said Williams.

"Sounds good to me. Give me a minute; I'm going to the ladies' room."

Wilson watched her as she walked away, and he could feel his heart racing, realizing that this situation could pull them into something that could complicate things. When Stella came back, Wilson was already working on his second Crown Royal.

"Hey, Wilson, did you ever think about being something other than a cop?"

Williams, temporarily intoxicated with feelings of passion, was taken by surprise at the question. He adjusted his focus to answer the question. "Well, when I was a kid, I wanted to be the Lone Ranger."

"That's kind of cool, Wilson. I heard they based the character on a real marshal, so that answer doesn't count."

"Yeah, as a matter of fact, he was a black frontier marshal named Bass Reeves."

"You mean to tell me the Lone Ranger was black?" said Kaboo.

"Yes, I do—look it up for yourself."

"Okay, I will. What about you, Wilson? Do you wear a mask too?"

The question hit Wilson head on, and he thought, "Yes, Stella, if you only knew."

To her, he said, "Get out of here, Stella. Why would I need a mask?"

"I don't know. You tell me," she said, pausing for a second, "Mr. Lone Ranger."

Williams shook his head, then finished the last of his drink and ordered another.

Stella knew she struck gold in her last remark but played it off, knowing as well as Wilson that their relationship could become complicated.

Back at the Second Precinct, Detective Le Kwok received a call from Officer Trenton, who was in the field.

"We just turned up two dead bodies," said Trenton. "I think homicide is going to want to see them."

"Why is that, Officer?"

"I think we just found your two suspects: a tall black male and a short, white female—both shot dead."

"Give me the location, and we'll be right down."

Le Kwok called Williams's cell, which went to voicemail; he called Kaboo but got her voicemail as well.

He murmured, "Not now, guys. Figures, Murphy's law—if anything can go wrong, it will." Le Kwok grabbed his gun from his desk and his jacket and headed out to the crime scene.

CHAPTER TWENTY-NINE

Hernandez had settled into her routine, watching the girls Shantel and Romara. She talked to them daily, teaching them how to be vigilant about their surroundings and what to look out for. The school itself was very secure; it had to be because so many of its students were the children of powerful, upper-class families. The Hummer she used to transport the girls was army green and bulletproof, just like the Lincoln. Although the girls did not require as much security as the ambassador, his mind was more at ease knowing that extra protection was being provided to his girls. Rollins had cameras installed on the Hummer, which allowed Hernandez to view the area from a monitor on her cell phone. On the hour, she would walk the perimeter of the school and look for anything out of the ordinary. Working with Rollins, she would check any spot that an assailant could attack from and any views toward the rooms where the girls had class. On her fourth walk around the premise, Rollins radioed her.

"Hey, Yolanda," he said, "I'm picking up unusual activity in the bushes about two hundred feet from you. My cameras aren't seeing anything, but there's heat motion."

"I'll check it out," replied Hernandez. She turned and moved toward the bushes, carefully scanning every bush and tree in her path, keeping her hand on the 9 mm strapped to her side. "Nothing is here, Rollins. Are you still seeing it?"

"No, maybe it was a dog or something."

Looking down, Hernandez saw fresh footsteps and some busted twigs next to the bushes beside the tracks. She turned to see what angle the spot provided, and looking toward the school, she could see the girls in class. "Hey, Rollins, we got work to do."

"Gotcha."

AFTER ENTERING XAVIER'S jazz club, Thursday, in the afternoon, Ed ordered a Jameson and soda and asked the bartender if Kwame was in.

"Who's asking?" said the bartender.

"Tell him Ed Miller is here."

The bartender called to the back office; moments later, Kwame came out. "Hey, my man, how are you?" he asked.

"Doing okay. I had some free time today, and I figured I'd hang out a bit, get my mind off work."

"Yeah, I hear you. Your taking time to relax is a good thing," said Kwame.

Motioning to his bartender, he told him to pour another drink, the same as Ed's, but this one was for himself.

"I had a real good time at your club," said Ed. "You really got a nice place here."

"Thanks, man. You're welcome to swing by any time, so what's shaking?"

"Just work and keeping things moving, but I wanted to see what you knew about the politics in this town."

"What do you mean?"

"In particular, the whole oil companies' offshore bidding wars. Do you know anything about the situation?"

Looking at Ed, Kwame could sense that something deep was going on. He took a sip from his drink. "Man, this drink is pretty good. What are we drinking?"

"It's Jameson and soda. So, can you help?"

"Why would I know about that? I'm a club owner; besides, sticking my nose where it doesn't belong could get it cut off."

"Fair enough. Sorry, I had to ask—it was worth a shot, because anybody who's somebody probably comes to your place. I know this is your town."

Kwame, still having a soft spot for soldiers and simply wanting to help, gave in: "Have you looked into the killing that occurred several weeks back? The victim's name was Dugan Metcalf."

"I know all about him. I was the one who found his body and reported it to Detective Williams, who is one of the investigators put on the case."

"No shit, so you've met Wilson?"

"Wilson? I see that you're on a first-name basis with him," said Ed.

"Yeah, Detective Wilson Williams—he's a hell of a cop," said Kwame, nodding his head.

"Well, he thought to put me on his person-of-interest list."

"Oh, why's that?"

"I'm running security for Ambassador Ballantyne, and somehow the ambassador figures into this mess."

"Do you think Ballantyne is involved?"

"No, not really—the ambassador seems to be upright and good. I think that he's working hard to do his job and that some outsiders are trying to gain advantages to the St. Vincent's oil rights. I think that Metcalf was dirty and that someone did some double dealings at Metcalf's expense."

"I see," said Kwame. "So you're all in the mix."

"You could say that. I'm in charge of Ballantyne's safety, but I could not care less about the rest of the crap going on—though I do need to understand it all. Bottom line, I need to keep him and his daughters alive and well."

"I'll see what I can find out. I'll ask around."

"I would appreciate that."

Both men ordered another Jameson and soda and chatted, getting to know each other better.

CHAPTER THIRTY

Detective Williams checked his phone calls and saw that Detective Kwok had left him a message. After listening to the message, Williams immediately called him back. "Hey, Le. I just got your message. Where are you?"

"Down at the docks, at the crime scene. We are at the seventh loading dock."

"We'll be right there."

The docks were a forty-five-minute drive from the grill where Williams and Kaboo were. They took the expressway, which cut through the downtown section and over to the far side of the island.

"Just when we come to the end of our wits, something turns up," said Kaboo.

"Yeah," said Williams, "I guess that sometimes we have to ease up and let go—that's when the breakthroughs happen."

"Yeah."

Williams and Kaboo arrived on the scene. The forensic team was already gathering everything they could find.

"Hey, Wilson," said Kwok. "Looks like two to the head for both victims."

"Anything else?"

"We found a key for a small jet boat docked here. Probably their getaway plan."

"Only someone had different plans for them," said Williams. "Let's find out who the boat is registered to. Any sign of a briefcase?"

"Not yet, but we'll keep looking."

"Good," said Williams. He turned to the forensics team. "Hey, how long do you guys need to identify the bodies?"

"Give us twenty-four hours," replied a man, who was part of the forensics team.

Detective Kaboo looked at the dead black male. She and Williams both knew who he was, but the woman was still a mystery. Looking around the surrounding area, she could not see any security monitors that might have captured images of the new killers.

Later that evening, Williams got a call from a man in forensics.

"Hey, Wilson. We started on the female victim, and looks like she had surgery—a pin implant. These implants have identification codes like a car's vin. The identification codes are required in case the manufacturers had to issue recalls on defective parts. We should be able to identify her through the implant."

"Great! After you find out who she is, lunch is on me."

The man from forensics laughed. "Yeah, I'll take you up on that."

CHAPTER THIRTY-ONE

Week Five

Following part of the team's normal protocol, which was to switch paths to and from the school to prevent attackers from plotting out a course of action against the team and its wards, Hernandez left the ambassador's home heading to the school, taking the girls in the Hummer, while Thornton followed in the open jeep. They had already decided that route C would be taken today.

"Okay, Rollins, we're on the move," said Hernandez, radioing in.

"All clear," replied Rollins.

"So, Thornton," said Hernandez, "when are you gonna shave that beard—you're starting to look like Abe Lincoln."

"You gotta get with the times, Hernandez. I'm waiting for you to grow yours."

Hernandez laughed. "Funny, man—I'll grow one when your momma grows one."

They headed south, down a residential street, which led out to a main road, the opposite way to the school. They would go down two blocks and then turn back and head down a parallel street, which would lead them to the school from another road. This road was safe enough for higher speed limits, so the team members could drive fast if they were ambushed.

At the school, the drop-off spot was unusually backed up.

"Thornton," said Hernandez, "you seeing this?"

"Yeah, looks like some police cars are in the parking lot."

"Keep your eyes open—this could take a minute. I may have to walk them out from here," said Hernandez. She switched over to Rollins. "What do you see, D?" (It was a nickname she had given him, which stood for Dennis, his first name.)

Rollins said, "Looks like a domestic thing going on; everything else looks okay, except a few of my cameras appear down."

"I'm getting out," said Thornton. "I'll go in with you."

"What a gentleman," said Hernandez. But her sense of humor was cut short—she caught a flash of something coming from the hill, about six hundred feet away from the school. Switching into action, she relayed to Thornton. "We've got something at six o'clock. See if you can get eyes on it." She hurried the girls into the school and into the school's security area. "Stay here until I get back," she told the girls. "Thornton, let's go find out what's up there."

Thornton nodded in agreement, both soldiers splitting up and moving double-time.

Rollins said, "You just scared the rabbit out of the bush—it's heading your way, Yolanda."

A man fled past her, about four hundred feet up ahead in the open bushes, and Hernandez flew after him. "Damn it! This guy is quick!" she said.

Thornton took off straight through the brush, hoping to cut the man off if he doubled back to the road just beyond the tree line. Hernandez increased her efforts, jumping over medium-sized bushes like a track hurdler going for a new personal best.

She gained ground on the man. Moving within striking distance, she lunged forward and tackled him by his knees. The man quickly turned on his back and thrust his right foot into the side of Hernandez's head, momentarily dazing her, which provided the man enough time to get up and away.

About then, Thornton had doubled back. He found Hernandez still shaking off the effects of the kick.

"Damn it," said Hernandez. "What did he hit me with?"

"Did you get a good look at him?" asked Thornton.

Looking down, she spotted something and picked it up. "No, but I think we have what he's been working with."

"Is that a camera?"

"Yeah, looks like this guy was taking pictures. Let's get this back to base and see what we have. I'll call Ed and tell him what happened."

"Rollins, did you get all this?" asked Thornton.

"No. Turns out those cameras that failed were not just an accident. They were in the direct vicinity of our mystery man's escape route."

Hernandez and Thornton reported to Ed later that day, handing over the camera they had picked up from the unknown man.

"Tell me what happened," said Ed.

The specialists went over every detail, and Ed dissected the events, all the way down to the kick to Hernandez's head.

"And the camera was his?" asked Ed.

"Yes, sir," said Hernandez. "I saw him carrying it when he first crossed my line of sight."

"Rollins, get this up on a computer; let's see what's on it," said Ed.

"Yes, sir."

The team viewed the pictures. There were some pics of several news stories that had just recently aired concerning the oil exploits in the Caribbean, but none of those stories were connected to the ambassador. There were also pics of the Dugan Metcalf crime scene and, oddly enough, pics of Ed in the Buerada Hotel's lobby on the day of the murder. The team was beginning to understand that they were dealing with a nosy, story-chasing newsman.

"He's a story chaser, like a lawyer, who is an ambulance chaser," said Hernandez. "Only instead of car crashes and law suits, he's chasing for oil."

"Exactly," said Marrio. "I wonder what we could find out from this guy if we caught him."

"Okay," said Ed, "let's find this guy and see what he's after; maybe doing so will provide information that could make our job a little easier. Rollins, see if you can match these pics with the news stories, then find out from the TV news channels who he is with. Get an address on him and any other oil industry–related stories he's involved in."

"Sure thing, sir," said Rollins.

"Hernandez, how'd this guy best you?" asked Marrio. "I've tested you myself—he had to be more than a newsman to do that."

"He was quick and agile, sir. It was as if he was some kind of athlete."

"Note that, Rollins," said Ed. "That detail might help us identify him."

"Yep, got it, sir."

Ed thought about a guy he had seen in the Buerada Hotel's lobby on the day of his finding Metcalf's body. Ed remembered sensing something about the stranger that did not feel right. Could that have been the same guy? The man he had seen in the lobby was in real good shape, looking like a runner or soccer player.

Ed pulled Marrio to the side. "I want another man on Ballantyne's girls, watching them from the time they leave for school until they are back home and safe. Right outside the classroom. Free up Hernandez to check out anything that might not look right along the perimeters. Let's keep quiet about this newsman for now; I'll tell the ambassador about him later, once we get more relevant information," said Ed.

"You got it, bro. I'll make the call," said Marrio.

Marrio looked over at Hernandez and thought about how she had run that guy down, had tackled him, and had taken the blow to the head. She was not fazed by the whole scene. "She's a tough chick—no, correct that—a tough soldier," he thought. Hernandez confrontation and fight, reminded him of something that happened to him earlier in his life while he was herding cattle back on his family's ranch.

CHAPTER THIRTY-TWO

Marrio daydreamed about his past, back when he was young. After helping round up some of the cattle for an auction, Marrio started on the north ridge, where most of the cattle had been grazing. Pablo, his father, called to him: "Look up ahead. There are several of the bulls; go and get them, and don't run them hard—we've got to sell them."

"Yes, Papa," he replied. He shouted "Yeeehaaa!" and was off to round them up.

Pablo thought, "That son of mine…the fire in his spirit…what will I do with him?" Then he chuckled and steered the rest of the cattle down the slope.

Marrio had rounded up all but one of the bulls, and as he approached the last one, who they called Elvis, the bull lowered his head and charged Pepper, Marrio's horse. Marrio and Pepper instinctively veered to the left to get out of Elvis's way.

"So you want to play, do you?" shouted Marrio. He then pulled Pepper's bridle to the right, sharply turning him toward Elvis. He then kicked his heels into Pepper's sides, and together they sped forth toward the wild bull. Elvis had not yet turned around, and Marrio came up from behind and slapped Elvis's rump with his rope.

"Show me what you got—you overgrown beefsteak!" yelled Marrio, laughing. "Surely, with a name like Elvis, you can do more than that." His mocking tone seemed to infuriate the bull, as if he knew he was being taunted. Elvis then spit from his snout and scratched his rear hooves against the hill's soft dirt and charged Marrio, again missing him only by a foot as Pepper veered to the side. Marrio shouted, "Not bad, Beefsteak, but no cigar for you." Marrio then charged the bull, this time leaning over with his hat and brushing it all the way up Elvis's back and leaving it hanging on one of the bull's horns. Elvis snorted and kicked and snapped his head back, tossing Marrio's hat in the air. Before the hat hit the ground, Marrio had swung back and, leaning low off Pepper's side, caught it.

Elvis's eyes were now blood red; his huge frame was sweaty from the exchange. This was not the first time Marrio had antagonized Elvis, and it seemed the bull wanted revenge. With his huge frame, he spun around twice, as quickly as the first time, and charged Marrio, lowering his head. As Pepper veered to the left, this time Elvis stopped dead in his tracks, twisted his body hard to the right, and caught Pepper off balance. One of Elvis's horns pushed into Pepper's rear thigh, causing the horse to stumble and fall to the ground.

Marrio flew ten feet through the air, then crashed to the soft dirt. Elvis saw Marrio rolling on the ground, and his eyes were inflamed with fire. Sensing this was his opportunity to crush Marrio, he spent no time snorting or doing the usual dirt kicking—he ran hard and powerfully toward Marrio, with his head low to the ground.

Marrio was still groggy from the fall. As he tried to get up, he spotted Elvis out of the corner of his eyes, so he tried to get out of the bull's way but was not fast enough. Elvis's horn pierced an inch above Marrio's hip bone and came out the front, tearing and slicing through his muscles. The thicker part of the horn did not penetrate all the way into Marrio's hip, but he gasped from the pain. The opposite side of Elvis's forehead rammed into his body, causing Marrio more agony, and the bull violently flung his head upward. Marrio had to grab Elvis's other horn to keep from being shaken to shreds.

The pain was unbearable, and blood poured down Marrio's thigh as Elvis continued to toss his head side to side.

Elvis then seemed to run out of steam, giving Marrio a chance to do something. His mind refocused and went into attack mode, thanks to the adrenaline coursing through him. Releasing his left hand from Elvis's horn and balling that same hand into a fist, he slammed it into Elvis's left eye. The blow made a squishing sound, and Elvis grunted in pain. He flung Marrio straight up into the air, and Marrio landed hard on Elvis's back. He tried to hold on, but Elvis was way too sweaty and slippery.

He fell again to the ground, landing right beside Elvis's front hooves. Elvis then tried to kick Marrio, who tried to grab the bull's feet to keep from being trampled. The plan was not working, so Marrio rolled as fast and hard as he could to get out of Elvis's way. The bull turned toward him and again tried to kick him. Elvis's eyes lit up when he realized he was now positioned above Marrio. Elvis raised up on his hind legs, preparing to crush the boy under his hooves. Marrio saw that he could not get out of the way this time, so he braced himself for the inevitable blow.

Marrio heard a loud, deep thump, followed by a sharp crack. When he opened his eyes, he was stunned.

Before Elvis could deliver his killing blow, Pepper came up to Elvis's left blind spot and used his rear hooves to impart a barrage of vehement kicks, thrashing Elvis until the bull collapsed.

"Way to go, Pepper!" said Marrio. Holding his side, he forced himself up to his feet. Pepper, however, was not finished: he charged Elvis and raised up his front legs, bringing them down on Elvis again and again.

Marrio shouted, "Ondale, boy, come here!"

Pepper heard his voice and turned and trotted to Marrio. Elvis lay beaten and bruised. The close brush with death and the excitement of the fight had Marrio high and intoxicated. He felt so alive. He thought, "What a magnificent battle."

His thoughts, however, took a more practical turn when he calmed down a little. "Oh, but Papa is not going to like this," he thought.

He recovered from his injuries, and so did Elvis; they both ended up having a new respect for each other. Marrio talked his father into not selling Elvis because he admired the fire in the bull's spirit, which reminded him of himself, or maybe they respected each other as warriors. He never taunted Elvis again, and Elvis remained at the ranch to live out his life.

Marrio's thoughts returned to the present and to Hernandez. "Yeah, this woman has grit," he thought, and his respect for her grew.

CHAPTER THIRTY-THREE

Friday came quickly, and Crystal was up early, excited at the thought of the motorcycle adventure that lay ahead, wondering where they would go. "Perhaps we'll go around the outskirts of the island, head up the coastal highway, and stop off at some of the grills and beaches, or maybe visit the small fishing docks," she thought. They could go into the interior of the large island, to its mountainous region, and venture up into the wild parts, where they could explore the indigenous creatures that lived there. No matter where Marrio would take her, it was going to be wonderful just being with Marrio.

Nine thirty came, and Marrio pulled up to the front of the Buerada Hotel. He was wearing a black-denim shirt, black jeans, and black boots with silver studs. Hell Fighter roared underneath him. A couple walking into the lobby turned in curiosity, as did the bell captain and a lady with her Cockapoo dog; all of them fixated on the magnificent bike before them. Marrio shut the engine off and dismounted. He then nodded at the bell captain, whose name was Sam.

"Good morning, Mr. Sanchez," said Sam.

"Hola! How's it going today, Sam?"

"It's a good day."

"It definitely is. I'll be out in five minutes."

"No problem, Mr. Sanchez. I'll watch her. She's a beautiful bike."

"Thanks, man. I had her flown in from the continent."

He walked into the lobby, where Crystal was waiting; she had just finished her paperwork and was ready to go. Marrio had never seen her like this: she was dressed casual, wearing tight blue jeans, black boots, a head scarf and dark sunglasses. Her shirt left her stomach exposed, displaying her exceptional muscle tone. Her graceful beauty commanded his awe, making him even more excited for the day ahead. Looking at her, he thought, "This woman is off the chart!"

Crystal tried to act calm, but she was clearly excited. Marrio pranced in like an Arabian stallion flying high in the moment. Crystal's eyes lit up, and she could no longer hold her calm composure—she was a giddy schoolgirl meeting the captain of the football team. Marrio was no better: the more she smiled, the more he pranced.

"Hola!" said Marrio. "Are you ready for this?"

"Hola! Yes, I am," said Crystal.

Marrio turned toward the door. Crystal hopped to his side, and he reached for her hand, leading her out the door. Everyone present witnessed the electricity in the air as the two lovers walked toward Hell Fighter. Marrio got on first and then looked at Crystal as she climbed on behind him.

"Make yourself comfortable," said Marrio.

"My dad used to ride, and I loved it when he would take me with him."

"Well, since you're not a stranger to motorcycles, then you shouldn't mind a little speed. But don't worry—I won't go too fast."

"Fast is okay, as long as you're safe."

"Don't worry. With me, you'll be safe. I won't let one strand of your hair be harmed."

He fired up Hell Fighter, and she roared as he turned the throttle. Crystal could feel Hell Fighter's power under her body as her thighs hugged and caressed the sides of the seat. She wrapped her arms around Marrio tightly, and the adrenaline surging through her made her feel more alive and excited. She drew closer to Marrio and held him tighter. Marrio could feel her as she embraced him, and he smiled. Lifting the kickstand, he let Hell Fighter roar again; then he released her, and they sped off.

Sam, the bell captain, watched as they rode off, looking until the sound of the roar faded and until they disappeared out of sight.

THE COOL AIR blew against Marrio and Crystal, as they rode toward the mountain region of the island. They felt exhilarated with each passing moment. Marrio took in the view of the dense woods lying before them, seeking out a trail that might lead to the top. As they plunged into the plush green landscape of the forest before them, the sounds of the city faded, and the signs of city life vanished. He slowed Hell Fighter down as they journeyed higher, and the engine, now only purring, allowed the natural sounds of the forest to be heard. Monkeys and parrots twittered and squawked in the surrounding trees, probably communicating about the noisy intruder.

It was darker now as they went deeper into the forest, and Crystal looked up through the tops of the trees, catching glimpses of the sun as its rays found their way through the dense vegetation above. Mystery lay ahead, and they were seeking it, climbing higher and higher on the tallest mountain on the island. They stumbled upon a waterfall, where Marrio brought Hell Fighter to a halt, guiding her over to a small and open area that was near a small lake of water at the foot of the falls. They paused to enjoy its powerful presence. They both dismounted from Hell Fighter and walked closer to the magnificent body of water before them.

"Nice" said Marrio. "This is beautiful. Have you ever been here?"

"When I was a child, my father would take my mother and me to the mountains, but we never ventured to this side or this high in them."

"So, you have never seen this waterfall before?"

"I have not."

"Was your dad from the island?"

"No, he was French, from Bordeaux, a city."

"And your mom, where was she from?"

"My mother was from Pointe-Noire, a port city in the Republic of the Congo."

"So how did you end up here?"

"You ask a lot of questions, don't you?"

"Hey," said Marrio, holding up his hands as if he were at gunpoint, "I just find you so interesting, and I want to know more about you."

"Well, my father's family were wine makers from Bordeaux, but my father had a different dream. He wanted to travel and see the world, so he joined the French Navy. In one of his tours, he came to Pointe-Noire during the Congo Civil War, where he met my mother. She was very beautiful and educated, and she worked in the oil industry. They fell in love and were married. He brought her back to France, where I was born, but still not wanting to grow wine vineyards, he heard of Bastalayo and brought us here. And you, Marrio? What about your family?"

"My family? I'm a third-generation American. My great grandfather was from Mexico. His ancestors were a mix of Aztecs, sub-Saharan Africans, and Spanish conquistadors. My mom's ancestors are a mix of Mexicans and whites from Texas. We were ranchers on the outskirts of San Antonio. My dad was a rough and tough cowboy, and he met my mom at a rodeo. He had to go through four of her brothers until he could marry her. They were pretty protective of their only sister, but my dad was determined to make her his bride."

"Sounds romantic," said Crystal.

"Yeah, I think it is a good story."

Crystal noticed the happiness on Marrio's face as he reminisced about his past. When he looked back, he saw that she was so inviting. He put his arm around her waist and pulled her slowly to himself. She did not resist, and they embraced, their lips coming together.

The moon made its entrance after the sun settled. Above them, a small family of monkeys witnessed the reciprocity of feelings.

"SARGE YOU HAVE a call" said Hernandez, handing Ed the land line.

"Ed Here". "This is Roy Preston, "Roy! Roy Preston", exclaiming in a suprised tone. "Man, it's been a minute, how are you?" Doing fine Sir, everything is great." Excited to hear from Roy, they served on the same squad in Afghanistan: and had gone through quite a bit of action together."

It had been at least ten years since Ed had seen him, now recollecting he asked, how is your wife Margaret and you have a daughter right?" Yeah, Cindy, she's twelve and we had two boys since I saw you, Charles and Phillip. Ed paused for a moment taking in the news before replying, "You're kidding! That's great." Pondering how Roy had contacted him, he asked, "I thought you were getting out of the service are you still enlisted? Said Ed. I thought about it, but when we found out we were pregnant with Charles, I decided to stay on a little longer for the money, so here I still am, also I'm your new guy." "This got Ed's attention and thinking, this work is too dangerous for a family man. Trying to express his concerns, hoping to persuade Roy from taking the assignment, Ed pressed

Roy to reconsider, but failing. Roy was adamant about taking the job. Ed sadly yielded "OK, I'll get you set up and have Specialist Hernandez and Thornton get you up to speed on what we are doing out here." Handing the phone back to Hernandez, giving her instructions to take care of Roy, he then walked into Rollins office, not feeling good about the situation.

CHAPTER THIRTY-FOUR

The team was two months into the mission, and no more incidents had occurred. Somehow, the mystery man with the camera had managed to stay a mystery. It appeared he worked through another reporter, who refused to reveal his source. Legally, the reporter did not have to, and Ed eventually decided that the man was not a threat to the ambassador—just an aggressive newsman trying to get a story. The ambassador followed his normal routine: he would get his girls ready in the mornings for their day then would head directly to the embassy to do his work.

The following Friday was a big day for Shantel and Romara. Every year, the private school they attended had a special bonfire event. This was a big thing for the students, and if a student were to miss it, that student would be devastated. At least that was the perspective of the ambassador's girls, when they gave their take on it. Sanchez and Hernandez would watch the ambassador that night, and Thornton and Ed would go with the girls. Rollins, as usual, would have eyes on everyone.

Friday rolled around, and Ed had explored quite a bit of the island by that time. He especially loved the beach, where he spent time in the morning, running on the sand or taking quick dips in the ocean before checking in for duty with the ambassador. On that Friday morning, he thought, "I've got to keep an eye on the ambassador's fifteen-year-old twin daughters tonight. This bonfire on the beach should be quite interesting. I'll probably get to scare the heck out of the young boys, who are probably on hormonal overdrive. The ambassador's daughters, though young, certainly are physically ahead of their time and quite pretty and adventurous. Double trouble for sure."

Later that night, Ed's predictions turned out to be accurate. He ending up having his hands full: a couple of boys in their late teens, both from powerful, upper-class families, zeroed in on the twins. When their hands started to go where no hand should go at their age, Ed stepped in, causing some embarrassment; however, things mostly worked themselves out, and Ed had Thornton in the ambassador's limo come at half past nine to pick up the girls.

Ed watched the limo as Thornton drove off, and then he turned and looked down the beach. "Whew! With all my training, I never saw that one in the manual," he said to himself. He laughed for a moment before walking down the beach a bit, to an area that was isolated. The moonlight shined brightly and reflected off the white, glassy sand, setting a backdrop for what lay ahead.

Ed was always prepared, being a seasoned soldier. He caught movement out of the corner of his eye, down near the water, and he turned quickly to see what was there. There *she* was. "Wow!" he thought, feeling breathless. It was as if he were being set up.

The moonlight reflected off the beach; the waves of the ocean rippled up on the sand; the cool breeze blew past Ed—and standing amid it all was a woman, the most beautiful creature Ed had ever seen, right there in front of him, dancing in the sand, humming some enchanting, melodic song. His heart leaped; he felt as if he had been hit with a thunderbolt. The world became unreal to him. He did not even know her, so how could she have such an effect on him?

As Ed gazed at her, he wondered, "Perhaps she lives around here. Maybe she's a tourist—no, she has an island air about her. Perhaps she's the daughter of a local businessman or the daughter of a fisherman."

What Ed could not have known was that her grandfather had been a fisherman, and without a doubt, she had caught this one without even trying. She turned and looked at Ed and smiled, then turned and walked away. He watched her disappear into the night, not quite knowing what to think. His mind quickly jumped to wondering whether he would see her again. "Man, I sure hope I see her again. Yeah…" he thought.

ED ROSE EARLY as normal, and went for his run through the neighborhood and through the park where the people had cheered for him as if he were Rocky. On this particular day, he was feeling a little tight, so he stopped to stretch out. Looking toward the hill, he caught a glimpse of a woman. She was walking a small dog and heading away from where he was. He could sense something about her but could not quite verbalize the feeling. Dismissing it, he finished his stretch and continued his run, heading through the park and down to the beach, then back up the main road that led to the local stores.

He stopped at a small grocery store to pick up a few Red Bulls. He walked in with his wallet in hand, and *she* walked out. He was blown away with her beauty, which caused him to drop his wallet. Usually, he was not at all shy with the ladies, but for some reason, this one had a special effect on him. He was too nervous to start a conversation with her, not wanting to sound awkward or forward.

The woman picked up on his trepidation, and Ed knew that she was silently laughing at him. She thought him to be awkward but cute. She noticed he was wearing military shorts and a shirt that fit him tightly, displaying his ripped, muscular body. He fumbled at trying to start a simple good-morning conversation.

"Good-morning-what-a-beautiful-day-today," he said, rapid fire.

She laughed and replied, "Yes, it is."

No more words came to him; an invisible hand was clamped around his throat. The woman slowly walked on, glancing back briefly, but Ed had not answered the bell. He thought, "What just happened? This is not me—I'm a lady's man but *froze*." He could not believe how he had reacted.

The following day, he saw her again at the park, while running on his normal route. Trying to act smoothly and keep his composure, he gave her the following lines: "Good morning. I'm fine. How are you?"

She answered, "I'm fine as well."

"Me too," he said. In his head, he was screaming at his idiocy: "You fool! People have shot at you—bullets have whizzed by your head!—but *now* you lock up?"

And he kept running. There was something about her that reduced Ed to a little schoolyard boy. She made him terrified to say or do anything.

About a week later and after several casual encounters, Ed was determined to pull himself together and *do something*. As fate would have it, they bumped into each other again at the park. She was walking her small terrier, and Ed was off for the day, running as usual. It was about seven in the morning. Ed saw her up ahead and would reach her in moments. He was still quite nervous, but he slowed down to greet her. She looked him in the eyes, wondering if perhaps he had more to say this time.

Ed paused as, yet again, his words caught his throat. The moment was slipping away, and he knew she would walk on. He had to think fast, not wanting her to go; if she slipped away, then he would only go on pining for her with no hope of redress. As she began to walk away, he dug deep and called to her. "By the way, my name is Ed."

She turned back toward him. "Hello, Ed. I'm Angelina."

He took a few steps toward her. "Say, I know you don't know me, except for the few times we've bumped into one another, here and at the store, and that first time on the beach—that was you, right? I have to admit I've been rather clumsy at conversation, but I'm not normally like this. I was wondering about something, though: I have the day off, and I was thinking it would be really nice to spend it with you."

He was sweaty but sexy; every muscle in his physique protruded, and his six-pack stomach bulged against his shirt. His jawbone was cut and shaped like a true soldier.

"Is that so," said Angelina.

Ed put on one of his lady-killer smiles. "Yeah! I think this could be the start of something special."

She was beginning to see the confidence in him; he was quickly changing into something much stronger than the fumbling man she had first bumped into. She liked what she saw. "Special? Like what?"

"I mean that I really think you're something special, and I'd like to get to know you better."

She looked back at him and smiled. "So what's the plan, soldier?"

CHAPTER THIRTY-FIVE

The phone rang, and Detective Kaboo answered it.

"Hi, Stella. This is Ralph Parks from the FBI. I have some information for you. Detective Kwok called to see if we could identify your murdered hit men. Well, I'm glad to say we have names and info on both."

"Great!" said Kaboo. "What have you got?"

"The woman is Sarah Plaudine, and it appears she was under a witness-protection program. Several years ago, she testified against a big-time boss in the drug cartel. Turns out she was a pretty shady character herself. She was never convicted of any crimes but was listed several times as a person of interest in several murder cases, all involving gang activity. This all went down in Colombia. She's from Portugal originally and started showing up on the Colombian police's radar about nine years ago,"

"Okay, and what about the black male?"

"Yeah, his name was Reginald Dane. He wasn't on the Interpol list, but he did have priors in Colombia. A couple of breaking and entering charges and one for assault. He did time in a Colombian prison."

"Thanks, Ralph."

"Anytime, Stella."

And they hung up. Wiliams walked over to her desk. "Anything helpful?" he asked.

"Well, we now know who the two-dead people were. We just need to connect the dots."

Just then, Williams's phone rang. "This is Detective Williams."

"Wilson, it's Michael Klein, and I've got something for you."

"Do I need to go to you, or can you tell me over the phone?"

"I'm at the casino. Why don't you come here. I'd rather not talk over the phone."

"At the poker tables?"

"Where else! Let's say in twenty minutes."

"Twenty minutes is good."

Williams looked at Kaboo. "Looks like things are starting to happen."

Both detectives left the office. When they arrived at the Bastalayo Casino, Klein was sitting at his usual poker table. He was winning handily and had about five times more chips than anyone else at the table. Williams stood behind him to get a glimpse of Michael's current hand. Klein, feeling his presence, twisted his head up and back to see Williams. "Hi, Wilson. Give me a few minutes," he said.

"Sure, we'll be at the bar."

Klein finished his hand and then had the dealer hold his spot at the table. He walked over to the bar, where both detectives were waiting. "Can I buy you two a drink?"

Kaboo looked at Williams and nodded no.

"No thanks," said Williams, "we're on duty. So, what have you got?"

"Let's sit down over there," said Klein, pointing to a secluded corner booth. After they sat, he said, "I was chatting with some colleagues of mine at the office, and we happened to talk about Dugan and how the poor sap ended up the way he did. One of my colleagues knew that Ms. Balestra was seeing his buddy Thomas Mullins, who is a head executive in our department for oil-exploration development. He kept his affair on the down-low, except he told this one buddy, whose name I'd rather not reveal. I don't need this coming back to bite me or him in the butt. Anyway, this is really crazy. Dugan was seeing her too, and I remember Mullins was starting to talk down about Dugan. Mullins is a pretty intense guy and can become real aggressive. I have never seen him take crap from anyone. When news came that Dugan was killed, Mullins seemed happy that the guy was dead."

"What's your take on it? Do you think Mullins could have done it?"

Klein shrugged his shoulders. "I don't know, Wilson. You're the detective."

"Fair enough," said Williams. "Thanks, Michael. Hey, I'm curious about something: how much are those stacks of chips worth?"

"About eleven grand. I'm killing them, Wilson."

"Hey, one murder case at a time, and remind me never to play poker with you. See you, Michael."

Klein went back to his poker table, and the detectives left the casino.

BACK AT THE precinct, the detectives pulled out all the info they had gathered on the case and started to go over it, checking again all the persons of interest, suggesting possible theories, suggesting motives.

"I believe that Klein thinks Mullins was involved. Let's see what we can dig up on him," said Williams.

"Mullins and Dugan seeing Ms. Balestra? It's time to pay her another visit," said Kaboo.

"So, let's say Mullins was a jealous lover; why hire two hit men? If he is as intense as Klein believes, shouldn't it have been a crime of passion? Wouldn't he have plotted it out and done it himself?"

"Maybe he didn't have the stomach to do it himself," said Kaboo.

"If that is the case, then we need to connect him to our hit men. Let's see if we can get a match of his footprint to one of the footprints at the crime scene." said Williams.

"I'll call Kwok and have him do some digging."

Detective Kwok entered the office and waited for the two detectives to finish their thoughts. Leaning his backside against Williams's desk, he listened as the two detectives finished. The detectives eventually turned their attention to him.

"What's up?" asked Kwok.

"Ralph from the FBI called," said Kaboo, "and gave us the names of our two dead hit men. We also found out that Mullins might have been a jealous ex-boyfriend and Dugan the dead boyfriend. We need to see if there is any truth to the dual affairs. Find out what you can about Thomas Mullins and these hit men. Here's what we've got so far." Kaboo handed Le Kwok the latest pieces of info.

"I'll get right on it," said Kwok.

"Wilson," said Kaboo, "let's take a ride."

ANTOINETTE BALESTRA WAS sitting in her living room. Sitting on the table was a bottle of half-empty cognac OV. Her makeup was smeared; her eye liner had run down her face. Her eyes were blood red, not from the cognac but from the tears she had been shedding for the last few hours.

She held a picture of Dugan and her, which was taken on a speed boat, off the northern shore of the island. It was a selfie.

"Why did he have to brag to Tom about our relationship and piss him off? Such stupid machismo! I know he did it. He had him murdered, but how can I tell the police without exposing myself? My reputation and my career would be ruined. I could even go to jail if the company pressed espionage charges. How could I have let Dugan talk me into giving him Tom's computer-access code? What was I thinking? They will think I was in on it. Why did I fall in love with *him?*"

The doorbell rang, startling Antoinette. She did her best to pull herself together.

"Who is it?" she called.

The voice on the other side of the door answered, "Detective Kaboo."

CHAPTER THIRTY-SIX

As time went by, Sydney Ballantyne's was going to more and more meetings with the oil companies. The decisions about how the offshore rights would be divided among the giant moguls were now more defined. Also, the Grenadines' national elections were approaching. Ed was in constant contact with his team, as was the ambassador with his. Things had turned in favor of Mobil getting a larger share of oil rights. Still, Ed and his team were on edge and remained on full alert because they remembered the altercation with the two assailants, the men who Ed's team had killed at the strip mall. The team's intel suggested that the two assailants were linked to an antigovernment faction in the Grenadines. Ed, however, wanted more-precise details on whoever was behind the attempt on the ambassador's life.

Sticking his head into Sydney's office door, "Ambassador, "have you got a minute?" said Ed,

"Sure, what's on your mind? Come in."

"My sources believe that the assassination attempt originated from your country, from an antigovernment extremist group. I'm not sure if I buy that theory. What doesn't add up is why they would come after you."

"Honestly, I've thought this over and over, and it makes no sense to me either. If I were dead, I would simply be replaced. It would delay the negotiations, but at this point, the outcome would be the same. At first I thought there could have been heavy players involved in the attempt, but I have changed my mind about that."

"So, what would this antigovernment group gain from your death?"

"Money? How about money? Every one of these factions needs money. Perhaps the assailants were just acting as mercenaries and doing someone else's bidding."

"Okay," said Ed, "so if we look at it that way, then who would want you dead for other reasons? Who could afford to pay for the hit and have the connections to get the attempted killers?"

The ambassador pondered over this for a moment; while thinking, it dawned on him that the day of the attack was the same date as the Cotillion Ball—that is, when he had finally won over his beloved wife. That ball happened so many years ago, and although the dates of the Cotillion Balls changed from year to year, the date of that fateful night had not escaped him: on that night, he not only won the heart of his one true love but also gained a mortal enemy for life. What was he doing now? Could it be after all these years that an old grudge was coming back to haunt him? Romeg certainly had the motive and the money, but connections with antigovernment extremist groups?

Ed could clearly see that the ambassador was having a revelation: the man's eyes narrowed and squinted sharply, and his hands formed fists.

"So, it's not over," said the ambassador. "Have your people check out Romeg Thomas."

"Romeg Thomas?"

The ambassador explained all that had happened between Romeg, Alicia, and himself, while Ed patiently listened. The more Sydney talked about it, the more he became convinced that he was on the right track.

"Okay," said Ed, "this is something. I'll check it all out and let you get back to your work."

Both men nodded to each other, as Ed left the office. Looking through his telephone log, the Ambassador picked up the phone and dialed a Grenedine number, to a person he helped out of a very messy situation and owed him a favor. "Hello" a voice sounded out. "Hello, this is Ambassador Ballentyne, how are you?" " I am fine Ambassador, it has been a long time since we last spoke" said the man. " Yes, it has been a while. You remember what I did for you?" said Sydney. "Yes, Of course, and I am very grateful." the man responded. "Now, you can help me, I need a favor." "Of course, Ambassador, what is it? " I need you to find out the location of Romeg Thomas. I need this to be kept discreet and he must not catch wind of it. Can you do this? asked Sydney. " I can do it. Shall I call you back at this number?" asked the man. That will be fine, I will look for your call, goodbye" and Sydney hung up.

CHAPTER THIRTY-SEVEN

It was now the third month into the assignment, and the Ballantyne family were all at home. The girls had the week off from school, and the ambassador decided to work from home to spend more time with them. Hernandez and Thornton were assigned to watch them from the base they had set up for the surveillance operations. Rollins was given a few days off to get out and see something other than the base's walls.

Hernandez grabbed a couple of sodas from the fridge and then went over to where Thornton was monitoring the surveillance screens. She plopped down in a chair beside him. Handing him one of the bottles, she pulled the cap from hers and turned the bottle up. Turning her attention to Thornton, she asked, "So what's your story, Randell?"

"What story? Do you mean my life?"

"Yeah! You're from Idaho, and I'm from New York City. Life's a little different in both places."

"You don't say!"

"So did you grow up on a farm or a ranch or back in the sticks or what?" asked Hernandez.

Thornton looked at her, his eyebrows rising. "Back in the sticks? So is that how you see me? No, I grew up on a farm not far from Boise, Idaho. You do know that's a city, right?"

Hernandez chuckled. "Come on, man—you got cities out there? Man, your cities are probably suburbs to me."

"Yeah, I guess so, since you're from NYC. How did you deal with all those people? People in front of you, people behind you, people on top of you, people underneath you—having all those people around me would drive me crazy. Give me wide-open spaces any day."

"Yeah," said Hernandez, shrugging, "the congestion is crazy, but we handle it. So you're a farm boy!"

"Yep, I'm a farm boy; I grew up milking cows and driving tractors. I did a lot of hunting and fishing. That sort of life may sound boring to you, but it wasn't for me. I loved it."

"Cool, man. Maybe I should envy you."

"You know," said Thornton, "I spent a lot of my time with my dad. He was always teaching me things."

Thornton looked down at his boots; then licking his finger and wetting it, he wiped a scuff mark from his left boot. He continued to reminisce about his childhood: "I remember the first time my dad took me hunting. We were chasing rabbits."

"Aww, man! You went after the poor, little rabbits!"

Thornton shrugged. "Hey, that's what we did."

"I'm only messing with you, Randell. Go on, tell me more."

"My dad put a sixteen-gauge shotgun in my hands and said, 'Let's go, son. We're going hunting.' He had taught me how to shoot a twenty-two-caliber rifle when I was ten years old and let me practice with a 410-gauge shotgun from time to time. I was twelve on my first hunting trip. Man, was I excited."

"Yeah, I can imagine. So what happened?" asked Hernandez, who was not kidding around. She was genuinely interested in the story and was listening closely.

Thornton was excited to tell her the story. He found Hernandez very interesting, and this was the first time they really sat down and talked to one another on a personal level. He went on with his story: "Well, like I was saying, he put a sixteen gauge in my hands, but I was a little scared to fire it because I didn't want it to dislocate my shoulder. You know, you hear these guns have a kick, but you really can't know how bad it is until you fire one."

"Yeah, I remember the first time I fired a gun; it was a twenty-two caliber. I was scared and didn't know what to expect—the adrenaline was a trip. So what happened?"

"So, we were in the brush and trying to flush out rabbits and pushing our way through. My dad led the way. I had the trigger fully cocked when I should have had it half cocked. It was a double-barrel sixteen gauge, just like the 410 I had practiced with. So, I was pushing the brush away with the barrel. My dad had already taught me that doing so was a no-no, but I didn't listen. My dad stepped off to the right while I moved forward, and I didn't realize I had my finger on the trigger."

"Aww, man," said Hernandez, "are you gonna tell me something crazy happened?"

"Hey, this is a true story—I am not lying. What happened next must have been divine intervention. During our time in that brush, my dad was right in front of me, but as soon as he stepped out of the way, I tripped on something, and my shotgun went off. It flew straight back and out of my hands, and dirt and brush in front of me exploded everywhere. It seemed as if my dad jumped twenty feet in the air. He looked at me, and I had never seen him so scared—but he was scared for *me*. He frantically checked me all over to make sure I was okay. Twice he yelled, "Are you all right?"

Rabbits were running out from everywhere. We didn't catch a thing that day."

They both laughed.

"Dang, Randell—that could have been your dad. There is a God, and he surely was with you two that day."

"Yeah, but guess what! after that, I never disrespected any weapon again."

Hernandez laughed. "All that and no rabbit stew."

They laughed together, again.

"But we went out a week later, and we got fifteen rabbits, and six of them were mine."

"Not bad. So, that's it, country boy?"

"No, we did a lot of things, as I was saying—fish, farm, ride horses, and chase girls."

"Oh yeah, I can see you doing all that."

"Yup, I had my share of ladies. I don't have any of those city-slick lines you might hear in NYC, but I got my skills."

"All right, I'm feeling you."

"Yeah, we threw our shindigs, and we did a lot of line dancing—which I was really good at. So, what do you do? You into salsa dancing or what?"

"Yeah, that and more. I got moves that would bring you to your knees."

Thornton looked at Hernandez and saw more than just a soldier. He saw the intrigue about her. She was strong, smart, and beautiful and had big brown eyes and smooth, well-developed muscle and tan skin. She had his attention now, and he was feeling her. "Yeah," he said, "I can see you in a hot dress and on the dance floor, kickin' it like Jennifer Lopez and showing off."

"If I put on a dress and heels, you couldn't handle it, Thornton."

"Yeah, right! You're underestimating this country boy. Why don't you teach me your moves, and I'll show you mine?"

Hernandez moved closer to Thornton, to where her lips were so close to his.

Thornton was excited, anticipation coursing through him, making his lips twitch. "Oh yeah, baby!" he thought. Her breath caressed and tickled his mouth and cheeks, causing his excitement to rise. "Oh yeah, baby!" he thought again. He imagined the pressure of her lips against him, and he waited. But Hernandez only pulled back and smiled.

"Gotcha!" she said. "I bet you thought you were about to get lucky."

Thornton was in a dazed state; then he realized he had been toyed with. "Oh, that's cold, Yolanda, and here I thought you had the hots for me."

Hernandez thought, "I do," but she did not want to reveal her feelings just yet.

Instead, she said, "In your dreams, Thornton."

CHAPTER THIRTY-EIGHT

"So, you got the girl?" Ed asked Marrio.

"You all right with that" he responded.

"Sure, man, I could see from the moment you two met that there was fire."

"It just happened," said Marrio. "I just felt her right away. But I know you were talking to her before I got here."

"No, man, it isn't like that. I flirted, but that's all. You are my brother, and I'm happy for you. Besides, I met this other woman. Man, she is something else," said Ed.

"Oh yeah? When did this happen?"

"It was really bizarre. You remember that night I watched the twins at the bonfire? After I sent them home with Thornton, I decided to walk down the beach. I came to this quiet, isolated spot, and there she was. It was crazy. She was dancing barefoot by the water, wearing just a white bikini and humming some melodic song. I have no idea what song it was except it sounded beautiful. Her long and dark hair blew freely in the breeze. She had these incredible brown eyes that pierced right through me. I was frozen. It was like time stood still as she walked by me," said Ed.

"Was it in slow motion" asked Marrio?

"Yeah! Why do you ask that?"

"The same thing happened to me. Man, what is it with these women here? Do they have our number or what? It's as if this place is having some kind of Bora effect on us," said Marrio.

"Yeah, some players we are!" said Ed, and they laughed together. "So look, Marrio, I'm going to take her out to Cymbal's this Friday; it's one of Kwame's clubs. So you have the ambassador covered?" asked Ed.

"Yeah, I got it. I'll put Thornton and Hernandez around the perimeter, and I'll stay in with the family," answered Marrio.

"How about Thornton and Hernandez, eh? Something is going on there," said Ed.

"I sense it too," said Marrio. "I'll keep an eye on them and make sure that whatever is brewing doesn't affect the mission."

"Who's going to keep an eye on us?" said Ed, chuckling.

"Hey, I watch you, and you watch me," said Marrio.

"That's dope. All right then."

They both laughed again, and the day moved on.

ON A FRIDAY evening, just after the sun had gone down, a steel-gray Dodge Challenger—fully loaded with a Hemi V8, its double black stripes looking sleek across its center—pulled up to the driveway of the beach home of Lucius Sucoy. Seagulls were sitting on the branches of the tropical trees, which swayed side to side in the night breeze blowing across the area not far from the house. As always, the seagulls were searching for food.

The driver's door swung open, and Ed stepped out, wearing a black and gray leisure suit and a pair of black Bruno Magli Alfanzo shoes. The shirt's short sleeves made room for Ed's silver, high-end

Omega watch, which glistened under the light coming from the porch. Around his neck was a silver cross given to him on his eighteenth birthday, a gift from his mother, one that he never took off. Ed Miller was ready.

As he approached the front door, the voice of an elderly man called out from the side of the porch. "You must be Sergeant Miller."

"Yes, I am."

"Angelina has told me about you."

"I hope it was all good things."

"Oh yes, only good things. I'm Lucius Sucoy, Angelina's grandfather," said the man.

"Pleasure to meet you, sir," replied Ed.

"Go right in, young man; she's expecting you."

After walking into the house, Ed found himself in a large living room filled with elaborate furniture displaying a white and tan decor. A large gold fan hung from its ceiling. The window blinds were wood shutters, tan in color, and quite elaborate also. On one wall, Ed saw family pictures. One showed Lucius as a young man with a woman, presumably his wife. Another picture showed him, a little older, with two young girls. "Probably his granddaughters, Angelina and her sister?" thought Ed. In another picture, a man was dressed as if he was from the East Coast. He had a back-east flair about him. With him was a beautiful woman, and she was holding the same two young girls in her arms. "That must be Angelina's mother, father, and sister," thought Ed. He was blown away by the mother. She was a bombshell, so it was no wonder that Angelina was so beautiful.

Ed heard someone behind him, and when he turned around, there she was again. Wow! On a scale of one to ten, she was every bit a ten. She was wearing a sleeveless red-hot dress, which settled right above her knees. Her matching Christian Louboutin red-bottom shoes set it off, adding even more splendor to her appearance, making her seem taller and more slender. As Ed's eyes traveled up her body, he saw her long, perfectly shaped legs, which disappeared under the soft red dress, giving way to the mesmerizing curves on her body. Her appearance would be enough to conquer even Alexander the Great. Around her neck was an eighteen-karat-gold necklace, with a half-carat diamond on a pendant, which was given to her by her grandfather, Lucius Sucoy.

She observed Ed's obvious pleasure. When his eyes met her big, bright, gorgeous brown eyes, she said, "Do you like what you see?" She turned slowly around, allowing Ed to take in all of her beauty. It was an overwhelming moment of pure delight. Ed almost felt it sinful to find so much enjoyment in looking at a woman.

He smiled. "I do. I like it a lot, yeah—wow! You are beautiful."

Later, Ed parked the Dodge Challenger at Cymbal's front entrance, at about eight o'clock. Two valet attendants ran to open both doors of the car. Ed stepped out, showing off his Bruno Magli shoes. Ed looked around and could see Tindale's High Tide Seafood, an exquisite restaurant sitting in the middle of the block. On the other side of the restaurant was Kainas Fashions, an eloquent shop for ladies.

Angelina stepped out of the car, and the attendant, suddenly dumbfounded, stared as her long, slender legs came into view. She stood up and waited for Ed to come around the car and escort her into the club, which he eagerly did. When they walked into Cymbal's that evening, the music was jumping. The DJ was a tall, heavyset man, who was wearing a rather large, white-brimmed hat and a multicolored shirt, which fit him loosely. His two front teeth were gold plated. The left one had a small diamond in it. He spoke fast, with a raspy voice, and sometimes slowed a word or two down in the mix of his rap, seeking to grab his audience's attention.

The lighting in the room was a soft blue, and each table displayed a different centerpiece of artwork. Alongside each centerpiece, a small white candle burned with a shimmering flame, presenting just enough light for the people sitting at the tables to see one another. Each candle established a cozy, private feeling. At the center of the room, a fountain stood seven feet high, spouting water in an array of colors; in the bowl of the fountain, which was about ten feet in diameter, were statues of ancient warriors.

After checking out the club, Ed looked at Angelina, and then he scanned the room again and noticed that many of the people were looking at her and him. Ed thought, "No, not so much at me, but at *her.*" He again was struck by her beauty. She had the most amazing smile, so soft and welcoming, so perfectly shaped to speak her divine, spellbinding voice. She had to be the envy of every woman in the club, for all the men were gazing at her in awe. She was a work of perfection; Michelangelo could not have sculpted a prettier angel.

Ed had to pinch himself to make sure he was not dreaming.

After a few drinks and a couple of laughs, Ed led her to the dance floor. They danced several times to the exhilarating, fast-paced music, and the DJ continually shouted for everybody to get on the dance floor and shake it. After three fast songs, a slow song finally followed, and Angelina waited for Ed to lead, which he did. Holding her left hand, he drew her close, and his powerful, battle-hardened eyes softened as he looked into her soft, seducing eyes.

"I have to be the luckiest man in the world to have you here with me now. May I have this slow dance?"

She laid her head on his shoulder and said with a slow, sonorous voice, "Yes, you may, Mr. Miller."

The night continued, and Ed thought, "This is one of the greatest nights of my life," realizing for the first time that he was with the one person who was everything he had ever wanted. "She is the one I've been waiting for," he thought, every instinct inside of him confirming the impression.

Feeling high and in the moment, Ed felt that he should ask her more about herself. He held her close, and then he spoke into her ear. "So tell me, how did you become this beautiful person?"

"What do you mean?"

"It's obvious you're beautiful on the outside, but you are also beautiful on the inside. How did you get this way? Tell me about yourself."

"Oh! Okay, well, I was born here in Bastalayo and lived here until I was six. Then my mom and dad moved us to New York, where my dad was from. So I grew up in New York. My sister, Tina, and I spent every summer here on the island with our grandparents. We enjoyed the best of both worlds."

"Tina...I saw her in a picture in your grandfather's house. You grew up in the Big Apple, so now I know where you got your city wit. What else about you?"

The song ended, and Ed led her back to their table. Putting on his best etiquette, he held the chair for her while she sat. Her eyes followed him as he returned to his seat opposite to her, and she smiled. Looking around, he motioned for a waitress to clear the table of old drinks and then returned his attention to Angelina. "So, what else about you?" he repeated.

"Are you a journalist or something?" she asked, laughing mildly. "I see that you're determined to know everything about me. Well, there's really not much to tell. I was a good girl growing up—at least I like to think so. I had lots of friends, and my mom and dad kept us busy in various activities so that we couldn't get into trouble. While I was a junior in high school, my father began to prepare me for higher education, and after I graduated high school, we agreed I would go to New York University, where I eventually got my degree in business administration."

Ed listened to her story and found himself appreciating her more with everything she revealed about herself. "Your parents sound like wonderful people," he said.

"Yes, they are so special; I love them so much."

"How did you end up here? It must have been a big change for you, going from a city girl to an islander."

Her countenance turned sad as she thought about Ed's question. "During my second year in college, we discovered that my grandmother had breast cancer. It was hard on all of us. Mom stopped working and spent the next several years taking care of her."

"Oh! That had to be hard on your father. Were you real close to her? Forgive me—that's a stupid question."

"No, that question is okay to ask. Yes, we were. It was very hard finishing my final years of college because in the back of my mind, I was always thinking about how my grandmother was becoming sicker. Her illness was hard on all of us. When I graduated, I moved down here to help take care of her and my grandfather, as did my mom. When I arrived here, I studied nursing so I could be more helpful.

"I'm so sorry for your loss," said Ed. He reached over and placed his hand on hers as she started to tear up.

"I didn't realize I was still grieving," she said.

"I didn't mean to stir up these feelings."

"I'll be okay. You know, when she passed, I was relieved it was over. I knew she was in a better place, though I did struggle with feeling guilty. I didn't know if it was okay to feel the relief of it being over. The situation hurt so much when we went through it. Anyway, I stayed here after she passed on, and I got a job teaching. I also do volunteer work in my spare time at the cancer ward at Bastalayo Medical Center. And here I am. My mother returned to New York where my dad and sister were.

Ed ordered two more drinks, and they drank them. An upbeat song started to play, and he grabbed her hand and pulled her to the dance floor. "I promise to ask no more questions—let's just dance," he said.

She followed him to the center floor, and they spent the rest of the evening dancing.

CHAPTER THIRTY- NINE

L ater that week, Kwame used his cell phone to call Ed.
"What's up, Kwame?" said Ed.

"Friday was a blast, right? I saw you having a good time. Yeah, and your lady friend was the hottest one in the house—does she have a sister?" asked Kwame rhetorically.

"Yeah, but she's too young for you," said Ed.

They laughed.

"Look, man," said Kwame, "come back down to Cymbal's. I have some information for you."

"Are you there now? I'll come right now."

"Yes I am. Guess I'll see you soon," said Kwame.

Ed told the team that he was stepping out and told them to stay alert while he was gone. Jumping into the Dodge Challenger, which was parked next to Hell Fighter, Ed drove out to Cymbal's. When he arrived, he handed the keys to the parking valet. "Take care of her," said Ed.

The valet nodded and hopped into her and drove around to the side parking lot. Ed entered the club and walked immediately to Kwame's office, which was in the back of the club. He was sitting down behind his large black desk.

"That was quick," said Kwame.

"Well, you know, I like to keep it moving, so what do you have?"

"Do you want a drink or something?" asked Kwame.

"No, thanks. I'm working," said Ed.

"Yeah, of course, doing your soldier thing. How is the ambassador?"

"He's well."

"Good. So here is what's going on: the word is that two guys were killed at the strip mall. A black Lincoln was seen leaving the area. You wouldn't happen to know any pertinent details, would you?" asked Kwame, tilting his head, signaling that he knew what was up but did not want to say any more about it in words. He continued: "Well, they worked for the Landoza Fire Arms and Ammo Corporation. They worked security for a lot of their gun and ammo deliveries in Africa. Mercenaries, really. Landoza deals a lot with small, unstable African countries, selling to both sides—the government and the rebel forces."

"How do you know this?" asked Ed.

"I told you that I know not only this town but also everyone who knows anything occurring in the island's and the Caribbean's light and dark sides."

"Okay, so they worked for Landoza. I still have to find out who ordered them to do the hit," said Ed.

"Landoza is not part of the Grenadines. The company is registered in Venezuela as an arms company, but it has a facility on a small, Venezuelan-protected island not far from the British Virgin Islands. The men that are contracted by Landoza fire arms company, are freelance mercenaries, and there are more of them. They protect the arms shipments from gun highjackers during the deliveries.. Also, the offer went out for Ballantyne's head in the Grenadines, but no one touched it. Looks as if those guys were a second pick to make the hit. No one is saying who put out the hit, just that it came from the Grenadines," said Kwame.

"I'll have my man check it out. Thanks," said Ed.

"You're welcome."

Ed thought, "There is a hell of a lot to Kwame; I was lucky to meet him."

Kwame said, "By the way, we've got a hot show happening at Cymbal's next weekend. Why don't you come down and bring your lady friend? And her sister too," he added, laughing. "Just joking, man. You two look good together, though."

"I'll think about coming to the event. Thanks for the offer," said Ed.

Kwame put his head down, returning his attention to some papers on his desk, and Ed walked out of the office. Reaching into his pocket, he pulled out his cell phone and dialed Rollins.

CHAPTER FOURTY

"Rollins, this is Sergeant Miller. I need you to find out what you can on the Landoza Firearms and Ammo Corporation. I want to know any and everything about whom they hire to run security when they move guns in Africa. I'm talking about the mercenary ones. I want to know these guys' past employers. I want to know how many there are and who they know in St. Vincent and in the Grenadines. Get me addresses and numbers. Whatever you can get."

"I'm on it, sir. I take it that this is a top priority?"

"Yes, that is correct." "By the way, Detective Wilson Williams has identified the two hit men involved in Dugan's murder."

Ed stopped walking in the parking lot. The parking valet was just driving up with the Dodge Challenger. "Who did it?"

"A man named Tom Mullins, who was an oil manager for Mobile, had the hots for an executive of Royal Dutch Shell. She dumped him and hooked up with Dugan. She got played by Dugan, who used her to get this Mullins's computer passwords. Dugan stole sensitive information and planned to sell it to Royal Dutch Shell. I guess he didn't realize how jealous Mullins could be. Mullins came to the park confronted Dugan, per Williams report. It appears he showed up right after the other two suspects, but they didn't find the briefcase with him. He claimed there wasn't a briefcase, just Dugan. Now, check this out. You know that detective really ought to double encrypt his files. It was too easy getting into them."

"I'll be sure to tell him," said Ed, being sarcastic. "Go on."

"So, Detective Williams wrote in his report that Mullins killed Dugan. The woman turned him in, to save her own hide, and when the detectives caught up with Mullins, they found the gun that was used to kill Dugan". Ed's thought was, so the third set of footprints at the park were Mulligans. He would have fired his gun from his hip. This would acount for the bullet appearing to be shot by a shorter person. "Ed responded to Rollins statement "So, who met them at the docks to pay them off for the job and get the briefcase? Or so they thought, seeing that they both were wasted instead.

Rollins then added, "Dang, you gotta suck at your job when the person that hires you to do a job ends up having you hit instead. Crazy world we live in." "Okay, let's put a pin in that one and focus on our issue. Who hired the hit men who attacked the ambassador? There had to be four men. Those two in the building couldn't have gotten in that van and over the bridge that quickly."

"Do you think they will try again?" Asked Rollins.

"Good question. Depends on how much they are getting paid and whether they have been paid at this point. One thing is for sure: they know that it won't be easy and that they stand a good chance of ending up dead themselves," said Ed

"Okay, I'll find these guys, because that's what I do," said Rollins.

Ed laughed. "Okay, bad boy of toys, go get 'em."

It didn't take Rollins long to find out more on Dugan. By the time, Ed arrived at the base Rollins was already walking up to him. Sarge, you know Dugan met Ambassador Ballantyne, through his personnel aide. I was going over the Embassy surveillance footage, it showed his aide meeting Dugan first, twenty minutes before the Ambassador came outside and was introduced to him. Also, Dugan handed something to the Aide. It looked like he pulled a folder from a black briefcase. "Interesting Rollins, let's see what we can dig up on Sydney's aide". "Sure, thing Sarge" Rollins responded. Both men walked over to his computer and after an hour of searching the internet, Rollins found information going back to Sydney's University days. "Hey Sarge! look at this, "

"So, the aide Dupont was in the same University with the Ambassador" said Ed. Looking at a picture of Dupont posing with two other men all dressed in soccer gear. Ed wondered if he and Sydney knew each other. Scanning the names listed at the bottom of the article, Clarence Dupont was on the left holding his hand high in celebration, the man to the far right was a Ricard Pixon who was looking off to his side and the man in the center Romeg Thomas. Ed studied the pictures then turned his thoughts back to Dupont.

How did the attackers know we would take that route, and at that time, for a meeting with Royal Dutch Shell? Could Clarence Dupont be the someone working for them inside the embassy? "Could Dupont and Romeg be behind this?" Ed stored the questions in his mind, and would keep an eye on him.

CHAPTER FOURTY-ONE

A man well dressed and well postured, bearing the appearance of a rich and powerful man, sat at a table in Dewell's Restaurant, which was in one of the finer resorts in Kingston, the capital of St. Vincent. The man sported a high-end, two-button black business suit, a jet-black shirt, and a black and white checkered tie that was pure silk.

It was a quarter past twelve, and the dining room was filling up with people wanting lunch. The man appeared impatient, tapping his fingers on the table, repeatedly looking at his Rolex and toward the front entrance. With a look of relief, he spotted the person for whom he had been waiting: a woman whose eloquent appearance matched his own. Her clothing was at the higher-end of business casual, and she stood about five feet five and was wearing flats. Her hair was dark brown, cut short, and well styled. Clearly, she was a pretty woman, but she had a gruff persona about her.

"Hello, Romeg, were you waiting long?" she asked.

"No, Evelyn, I just arrived right before you," he answered, not wanting to sound desperate. "Did you and your lawyer look everything over?" he asked.

"Yes, and everything is in order," she answered.

The woman was Romeg Thomas's wife, Evelyn Thomas. Romeg could tell she was somewhat irritated. "So what's it this time?" he asked. "What's bothering you?"

"You, Romeg. Always *you*."

The waiter stood before them, holding out menus, and asked, "Will you be ordering drinks?"

"Yes, please," said Romeg. "I'll have a Johnnie Walker Blue on the rocks, and make it a double." He looked at Evelyn. "You want the usual?" he asked her.

"No, nothing for me, thank you. That will be all for now," she said, dismissing the waiter.

"So it's always me? How many times have I heard that?"

"Well, fortunately for the both of us, you won't be hearing that for much longer."

"Where is that drink? If I have to hear this again, then I need to be comatose," said Romeg.

"Funny!" said his wife; then she paused. "If you had truly loved me instead of clinging to that stupid fantasy about—"

"Don't go there, not right now. We'll just fight and not accomplish anything."

"Well, that's what we are doing anyway. Whether verbally or silently, we always fight. I thought that after her death, you might let her go. All I ever wanted was for you to love me. Me and only me. Why was that too much to ask?"

He thought about her questions and her desire. He softened up inside and thought, "Life is complicated, and seldom do we get what we want." He saw her vulnerability and could relate to her pain, for he had the same feelings for Alicia Ballantyne. He had loved her and always would, but she had chosen him—Sydney. Evelyn was a childhood friend, and they both came from well-to-do families that were powerful friends and allies. It was almost as though both families arranged and coerced them into marriage; however, Evelyn had no problem with it, for she had always loved Romeg.

"The divorce's financial agreement is very generous of you," said Evelyn.

"You deserve it. You've always been there. Things just did not work out, and we have changed over the years."

She gazed out of a large window that provided a view of the ocean and the crowded private beach, which catered to the wealthier tourists that visited St. Vincent.

She looked back to Romeg's eyes. She thought, "I believed that after the accident, I could win you back. Everything I did wore at my soul. I did everything to fight for you, and still I lost." She shook her head and then said, "It's over now, maybe we can find peace."

Romeg thought, "No, my dear, it won't be over until I get him. If my revenge costs me my life, I still will not be denied. Sydney ruined my life, and he will pay with his own."

"What's going on in your head? I sense you're up to something," said Evelyn.

"Nothing you need to be concerned with. I'll tell my lawyers that you approve, and they will set up a time for us to conclude our divorce."

"Okay. Well, I guess we are done here. Good-bye, Romeg." The soon-to-be ex-wife exhaled.

"Good-bye, Evelyn."

He was now looking out the large and scenic window, unable to look at her or think about the finality of the last fifteen years. As she rose and headed toward the entrance, the waiter returned. "Will you be ordering, sir?" he asked.

"Give me the grilled salmon and pilaf rice and another double. That will be all."

CHAPTER FOURTY-TWO

Dennis Rollins sat behind his computer desk and pondered about where he would start. After typing in the name Sydney Ballantyne on the keyboard, various articles showed up on his computer's screen. One article covered a recent ceremony in which the ambassador was the speaker for a school drive for endangered children, specifically those who were immigrants from the neighboring Caribbean countries. Some other articles covered his progress on the council board that was working on the oil rights for St. Vincent.

Rollins decided he would need to go back further and get an idea of how Ballantyne started. Rollins went back ten years, and when he had scanned down to the last five years, he pulled up an article that showed pictures of Sydney and his family at a political ceremony in the Grenadines. Sydney was standing tall and proud with Alicia, his wife, by his side. They were holding hands.

Sydney and Alicia had one of their girls on each of their sides. Sydney held Shantel's hand, and Alicia held Romara's. Rollins thought they certainly looked happy. He then wondered about what happened to Alicia. Rollins did a search for her name only, and an article appeared about the car accident that had claimed her life. The article read as follows:

Woman Found Dead

Alicia Ballantyne of St. Vincent was found dead in her car at 6:20 a.m. on Saturday morning. Mrs. Ballantyne, socialite and wife of Ambassador Sydney Ballantyne, was presumably killed when her car ran through the railing and over the cliff next to Mount Moyers Drive. Investigators are still accessing the cause of the accident. At this time, no foul play is suspected; however, alcohol and prescription medications may have been involved. Alicia, who was known to have a very busy public life, was seen leaving the St. Vincent Annual Cancer Awareness Charity Function at 11:55 p.m. on Friday night. Friends say she appeared fine and noticed nothing out of the ordinary with her.

According to the article, investigators suspected that Alicia fell asleep behind the wheel and veered off the road, over the cliff alongside Mount Moyers Drive. The lead investigator, Detective Wilson Williams, stated that the police were engaging in a full investigation and were not ruling anything out presently.

Rollins called Seargent Miller, and gave him the information he had discovered. "I want you to run this by Detective Williams. I'll call him and give him a head up" said Miller. Ed picked up quickly that Rollins skills were good, and it wouldn't hurt to have Rollins insight.

Rollins thought, "How strange. Why was a homicide detective handling an auto accident? Maybe that's procedure." He picked up his cell and called Williams.

"Hello, Detective Williams here."

"Detective, this is Dennis Rollins; I work with Sergeant Ed Miller. I was wanting to talk to you about a case you worked several years back."

"I'm listening, Mr. Rollins. What case was that?"

"Alicia Ballantyne's car accident."

"Okay, I see why you are interested. Why don't you come down to the station so we can talk in person?"

Rollins agreed to meet, and when arrived at the Second Precinct, he was escorted to Williams's office. Kaboo had stepped out for a lunch break.

"So, what do you want to know?" asked Williams.

"Well, Detective, if I overstep my boundaries, please let me know. As you are aware, someone is trying to kill the ambassador. I did some digging and came across a news article that covered Alicia Ballantyne's death. I saw that you were the lead detective put on the case. I noticed no foul play was suspected, but I was wondering if you at any time suspected anything peculiar?"

Detective Wilson Williams pondered the question for a moment before deciding to answer it. That case had bugged him from the very start. He remembered his hierarchy shutting it down because of the political ramifications at the time. It seemed simple enough. A woman had a few drinks, took some sleeping pills, stayed late at a party, and drove home, only to fall asleep behind the wheel of her car. But back then, he had wondered why his superiors had closed the case before all the protocol was thoroughly completed. Rumor had it that supposedly the superiors closed the case to prevent a scandal at a time when the deals for the St. Vincent oil rights were still at a delicate stage. Sydney was the glue that would hold the deals together, so he needed to be protected. "But how in the world did he work through it?" wondered Wilson.

"So, what do you say, Detective?" asked Rollins. "Will you help me?"

"Sure, but you've got to keep in mind that this case was closed and sealed shut by my superiors, so if whatever I tell you comes out, I will deny all of it."

"Understood. We operate in secrecy, so there won't be a problem."

Detective Williams told Rollins all the official information that was released to the public and then added what he suspected and why. "I never did a full investigation on the case. I was pulled off it, and it was given to a detective in another district. That detective's conclusion is what you saw in the official concluding notes—that is, Alicia simply fell asleep and crashed."

"What about the ambassador?" asked Rollins. "Does he know about the flimsy investigation?"

"No, I don't think so. He trusted the source and bought into the story. Besides, there was so much going on at the time, so there is no telling what he was able to take in."

"And what about you?"

"I wanted to examine that car. The scene of the accident was fifteen minutes from the charity event. I wonder how she fell asleep so soon after getting in the car."

"Where is the car now?" asked Rollins.

"Good question. Two years have passed, so it could have been destroyed by now. I'll have to look into it."

"No offense, Detective, but I think I can find it faster—with your help, of course."

"You're the computer geek, right?"

"Right!"

"I'll have to run this by my partner; nothing happens without her agreement."

"I understand," said Rollins. "Well, you know where to find me."

Rollins turned toward Detective Williams's office door and walked out and left the station., pulling out his cell phone, he called Sarge.

Sergeant Miller entered the Embassy building and walked into Clarence Duponts office, knocking as he entered. The aide was startled, but quickly regained his composure before speaking. "Hello Sergeant, this is a suprise. What can I do for you?

'Hello Mr Dupont, I need to ask you a few questions regarding the Ambassador."Oh! OK, what are they?" replied Dupont. "Before I ask, I just want to tell you, this is all just routine investigation, so try not to read too much into it. You went to St. George University, the same time as the Ambassador, is that right?" "That's correct Seargent." "Did you know him then?" asked Miller. "Not really, we were in different circles. I did know of him, and met him several times as we both pursued our politcal careers, but only interacted with him after he became Ambassador, and I took the job as his aide. Why do you ask Sergeant?" Again, Miller reassured the Aide this was simply procedure, "Of course, you know about the Dugan Metcalf murder, and because the Ambassador had business affiliation with him at the time of this incident, we have to talk to everyone involved." "ok," responded Dupont. "You introduced Dugan Metcalf to the Ambassador." "That is correct Sergeant" #You also met with him twenty minutes before introducing the Ambassador and Metcalf handed you papers. Did you know Metcalf before this?' asked Miller. Dupont was becoming irritated and nervous at this line of questioning. "Are you insinuating I'm involved in some kind of conspiracy?" the aides tone of voice now rising. Miller could see that he struck a nerve. "No, not at all, it's just my job to ask all the questions relevant or not." answered Miller. "No I did not know this Mr Metcalf." answered Dupont. "Again, let me assure you, this is all just procedure" said Miller. The Sergeant wasn't buying the statement that Dupont didn't know Dugan previously, but held off pushing the questioning, having gotten the answers he seeked through Duponts body language and response. Ed decided to wait and see what would develop and what the aides next move would be. "No harm intended Mr Dupont, I'm sorry I had to ask you these questions, just doing my job." "Good day, Sergeant." "You too, Mr Dupont" and Ed left the office.

CHAPTER FOURTY-THREE

After four months into the assignment, things settled down. Marrio managed to get Saturday free, while Thornton, Hernandez, and Rollins held down the surveillance of the ambassador and his girls.

Marrio, riding Hell Fire, pulled up to Crystal's home and waited for her to come out. The door opened, and she was promptly on time. Walking up to Marrio, she leaned over and kissed him.

"Are you ready for this?" he said.

"As ready as I'll ever be," she answered.

They were going to the Bastalayo Casino to share a night of fun, and Marrio was hoping to get lucky. Crystal, too, could sense the time had come. The black and powerful bike rolled up to the circled driveway of the casino. They hopped off and proceeded through the main entrance of the large, illuminated lobby of the building. Marrio glanced around, taking in the flamboyant appearance of its interior design. They walked passed a long line of poker tables, and one in particular caught Marrio's eyes. The game being played looked like a high-stakes game—at least fifty grand was in the pot. As he walked by, he heard the dealer say, "The bets on you, Mr. Klein."

Heading toward the craps tables, Marrio saw Ed and his new friend Kwame Taylor. Both men were dressed casual and were very much into the game before them.

"Isn't that Ed?" asked Crystal.

"Yeah, he's got a thing for the dice. Come on, let's see what's shaking."

When they got to the table, Marrio motioned to Ed to make room for them. Ed stepped over, allowing the two to squeeze in. He then introduced Kwame to them. The four of them enjoyed the action and excitement at the table, laughing as they showed Crystal how the game was played. When the dice got around to their side of the table, Marrio gave Crystal the dice to throw.

"I don't know how to throw these," she said. "I don't want to mess up all of these people's bets."

"Don't worry, baby," said Marrio. "It is what it is when you throw the dice. They all knew the risks when they laid their cash on the table. Here, let me help you."

Standing behind her, his body pressed against hers, and his right hand held hers with the dice in it. He showed her the flow of the throw.

"Throw them just like that."

The dice flew across the table. "Four!" shouted the table man. He placed the black disc on four while his assistant pushed the dice back to Crystal.

"Okay, baby, all you have to do is throw another four and we win."

They made a modest bet of twenty-five dollars on the bet line; however, there were several high rollers at the table, who were picking up the energy of the love couple, and everyone was having a great time.

"Okay, here it goes," said Crystal.

She shook the dice several times, building up everyone's excitement, and then let the dice fly.

"Winner four!" yelled the table man. The people at the tabled yelled exuberantly.

She rolled a few more points, and the people roared in delight to the points being made, before she finally crapped out.

"Pretty good, babe," said Marrio.

He then looked up at a large LCD monitor displaying shots of the beaches and ocean and many people parasailing. He looked at Crystal and asked her to go on one with him. She was not thrilled with the notion, so Marrio offered her a proposition: "Look, if I roll a seven with these dice, will you go parasailing with me?"

"Hell no! That isn't going to work—what's in it for me?"

"Come on, babe. How about if I don't roll a seven? Then you get to choose something for us to do."

"Okay—now we're talking! I'll tell you what: my favorite number is eleven, so if you roll an eleven, then I'll go. But if you don't, then I will tell you what we will do, and you must do everything I say." She gave Marrio a devilish look and handed him the dice. "Your turn, Mr. Magic," she said.

"You're on," said Marrio.

Everyone at the table overheard the conversation, and loving a good intuitive bet, they all threw money on eleven—tons of money. As a matter of fact, they bet stupid money—five thousand dollars lay on fifteen to one odds. If Marrio hit an eleven, the house would have to dish out seventy-five thousand dollars for just one throw. The table man, sensing the energy, called the pit boss over, who had already noticed and was on his way. After assessing the bet, he listened to a voice in his earplug and then nodded to the table man to proceed.

Being hyped, Marrio jumped up on the craps table and flung the two dice as if they were ninja stars. When Marrio turned back around, the pit boss gave him a crazy look as if to say, "Get the heck off the table, fool!" Marrio then looked back at Crystal and winked and jumped back down.

The dice smashed into the opposite end of the table. The first one hit a stack of chips and immediately landed and displayed a six. The second dice flew about two feet high, straight up from the table, and it seemed as if an eternity passed before it came down. All of the players' eyes were glued to it; they were all chanting and roaring, "Eleven! Eleven! Eleven!" When the dice hit the table again, it started spinning and spinning, further churning up the pandemonium at the table. People nearby ran to see what was happening. The atmosphere was electric, and all four friends were shouting along with the crowd. The second dice was finally slowing, and everyone's eyes became wider with anticipation.

It landed on five.

"Winner—eleven!" declared the table man.

All of the players went nuts. "What a magical moment!" thought Marrio. Even the pit boss smiled, knowing that he rarely got to see such excitement. The house had lost seventy-five grand, but the pit boss would be telling that story for years.

CHAPTER FOURTY-FOUR

Another week had gone by, and the job was the opposite of a movie—life with all the cool stuff taken out. The team, however, remained on high alert during the boring interim, and when action did come, it was quick and intense.

The Ballantyne girls were busy texting boys as they sat in the rear seat of the green Hummer. Thornton, as usual, followed in the jeep behind them. Hernandez had the new man Roy Preston, drive while she scanned the area as they headed home. She looked at her cell phone, which was connected to the cameras on the Hummer. The cameras did not miss a thing. Rollins had set them to send an alert whenever an irregular pattern showed up, and sure enough, Hernandez got a hit. "Slow down, Roy," said Hernandez. This was the new man's name.

Scrolling back the monitor, she saw that windshield of the car that was following Thornton was sending out flashes. "Roy, turn the corner here, then stop. I'm going to get out; then you keep going as planned. Tell Thornton I said for him to stay with you."

The Hummer turned the corner, and Hernandez leaped out. Thornton's car followed the Hummer as planned.

The car tailing them was a black Chevy, and it had been following them since they left the school. As it made the turn, Hernandez was waiting for the car with her 9 mm out; then she pointed it at the man's head and yelled, "Pull it over now!" The man in the Chevy was caught off guard; freaking out, he ran into the wall on the opposite side of the small side street. Hernandez ran to the driver's door and pulled it open.

"Get out! Get out of the car now!" she repeated.

"Okay! Okay! Don't shoot me!"

"You're the same clown that was taking pictures of the school."

"Yeah! I'm just a news cameraman. Just doing my job."

Hernandez already knew this but questioned him further: "and what job has you covering the ambassador's girls? Oh, and you kicked me in the head trying to get away."

"I'm sorry about that. You had a gun."

Yolanda thought, "I guess that's fair. I did have a gun." To him, she said, "Come here. Let's see what you look like up close."

The newsman moved closer. Hernandez threw a right hook—crack! She hit him on the side of his jaw. The man fell to the ground. "Dang, lady—why did you do that?" he said.

"You're lucky it's not the heel of my boot," said Hernandez. "You're coming with me. My boss has some questions to ask you."

"You mean Sergeant Ed Miller?" asked the man.

"So, you know him."

"I do. Actually, this is great! Maybe there's a story there."

Hernandez looked at him inquisitively, and they got into the camera man's now dented car and headed to the base.

CHAPTER FORTY-FIVE

Hernandez and the cameraman, David Reese, pulled into the driveway of the team's base. Rollins, seeing the cars arrive, called to Hernandez and cleared her to come in. Ed met them in the main room of the house.

"So you're our mystery man," said Ed. "Please, have a seat. You were at the Buerada Hotel on the morning when the Dugan murder was discovered?"

"Yes, I was," said Reese.

"May I know why?"

"I heard the call about Dugan's body over the police channel, which is one of my methods for finding leads and getting a jump on the competition. I hightailed it to St. Donte's Park. I saw you talking to Detective Williams, and when you left, I walked near the detectives and overheard them saying that they would keep an eye on you."

"Is that right?"

"Yeah! Well, my instinct for news was wanting me to follow you as well. That's why you saw me at the hotel. I also followed you to the embassy, and when I researched you and found out who you went to see, I put a few things together. I knew the ambassador was heavily involved in the negotiations for the offshore oil rights, and Dugan just happened to be in that business."

"So, you followed me. Spill it all out."

"Well, I'm a little cloudy on the rest. Maybe if you tell me something, it will help jar my memory."

"Oh," said Ed, "so we're going to play that game. Okay, why would someone want to kill the ambassador?"

"Sydney? That I don't know, except I remember his wife's car accident. She died in that crash. I pursued that case too."

"So, what did you find out?"

Reese rubbed his jaw, still feeling the effects of Hernandez's punch. He stood up and walked around a bit before speaking again. "I remember talking to some of the people that were at the event that night. My understanding was that Mrs. Ballantyne was a little upset. One of the people there told me she had seen Mrs. Ballantyne talking to an Evelyn Thomas, who was a socialite from St. Vincent. The police never mentioned any of this in its report."

"What about Detective Williams? Did he know?" asked Ed.

"No, he was removed from the case fairly quickly, and from what I could tell, some things were suppressed because of the sensitivity of the matters that involved the ambassador."

Rollins walked in at that time and, overhearing some of the conversation, interrupted them. "Did you just mention Evelyn Thomas?"

"Yea," said Reese, "that's the one."

Rollins pulled Ed to the side to share information with him. "I talked to Detective Williams. He wants to have a look at Mrs. Ballantyne's car."

"Does he know where it is?"

"He's working on locating it, and he'll tell us when he finds out—if I don't find it first."

"Okay, you let me know when you learn anything," said Ed. Turning back to David Reese, he asked, "Why were you taking pictures of the ambassador's girls?"

"I was collecting pictures for my story."

"And what is your story's angle?"

"This one we are working on now. Newsman instinct."

CHAPTER FOURTY-SIX

Rollins walked back into his surveillance room. At that time, Marrio, Hernandez, Thornton, and the new man, Roy, were covering the ambassador and the girls. Rollins came back into the main room, where Ed and David Reese were still talking. Ed gazed over at Rollins, who signaled Ed over to show him something.

Ed stepped away from David Reese and walked over to Rollins. "What's up?"

"I just got a call from Detective Williams. He checked the records on Alicia Ballantyne's car and where it was towed. It seems the car was removed from the salvage yard and was signed off by a Jay Snyder—of whom there is no record anywhere. However, there is a photo of him from one of the salvage yard's surveillance cameras. Williams sent it over. I'll check it out."

"Good," said Ed. "How long before you can identify him?"

"Williams is still working on it."

David Reese, leaning over to eavesdrop, caught wind of the conversation and asked to see the photo, which Ed allowed him to see.

"I've seen this guy," said Reese. "He was at the charity event, the night of Alicia Ballantyne's accident."

"Are you sure?" asked Ed.

"I'm a newsman—I'm trained to catch this kind of stuff. This man was in the parking lot with the limousines. He must have been a chauffeur."

"The more we look at this, the crazier it gets," said Ed. "I'll call Williams myself and tell him about the man in the photo. Looks like we are going hunting."

Ed said good-bye to David Reese and escorted him to the door. Reese asked about his car.

"Occupational hazard," said Ed. "The cost is on you."

David shrugged and then murmured, "Damn government."

WILLIAMS WALKED OVER to Kaboo, who was at her desk, doodling on a notepad. They were supposed to be assisting the North Town First Precinct with a new murder case, but ran the photo by her. "It seems our Sergeant Miller has discovered a few things of interest," said Williams. "He could be a good detective if he wanted to."

The detectives looked at the photo again.

"We need to find out who this Evelyn Thomas woman is and who this fictitious Jay Snyder really is," said Williams. "Let's see what else our soldier friend lets us in on."

"Yeah, there is some really freaky Aurora Borealis northern light energy floating around this guy."

A few days later, Ed's phone rang, and he answered it.

"Hello, Sergeant. I've got a real name for our man in the photo. His name is Floyd Rochester, I did some more research on him. He's the chauffeur of Evelyn Thomas, and she's a rich socialite from St. Vincent and the Grenadines."

"It's interesting, Wilson, how this all seems to lead back to the Grenadines. You know I appreciate the cooperation you've given me. I'll tell you as much as I can, but you know this is still government business we are working with here."

"Oh, okay. I know that we are on a first-name basis, but I guess that soon we'll be joined to the hip on this case."

Ed laughed. "God! I hope not—you're not my type, but you are growing on me. I'll get back with you; there's something I need to check out."

"Okay," said Williams, and both men hung up."

Ed thought, "It's time to talk to the ambassador."

CHAPTER FORTY-SEVEN

Ed called the ambassador's office. Sydney was finishing up a call with an oil executive of Royal Dutch Shell. Sydney was a little irritated because the executive was giving him an earful. The advantage had shifted back to Mobil, and Royal Dutch Shell was out. Sydney had been the bearer of the bad tidings, but the executive was trying to vent his frustration on Sydney. The receptionist called into the ambassador's office.

"Sergeant Miller is on line two," she said.

Sydney picked up the phone and asked, "What is it, Sergeant?" The tone of his voice clearly implied that he was perturbed.

"Did I catch you at a bad time?" asked Ed.

"I'm sorry," said Sydney. "I'm fresh off a nasty call. What's on your mind?"

"Who is Evelyn Thomas to you?"

"To me? Nobody. She is Romeg Thomas wife, and he has known her since they were kids. What does she have to do with anything?"

"Bear with me, Ambassador. I'm going to tell you what I know and then what I think happened to your wife."

"My wife? Sergeant what is going on?"

Ed told the ambassador all he knew about the night of the accident. The ambassador asked to see the photo of the man at the salvage yard. Rollins promptly sent it to Sydney's computer.

"This man is Evelyn's private chauffer?" Said Sydney. "Are you thinking he's involved and helped cover up something about my wife's car accident?"

"I think we are looking at murder," replied Ed.

Both men hung up.

THE AMBASSADOR REACHED into his desk, and pulled out what appeared to be an itinerary of Romeg Thomas. The man Sydney had helped, back in the Grenedines, owed him a large favor. Sydney had saved him from going to prison and placed him in a government job providing cyber security to the Grenedine gov't Internet systems. He was a computer hacker, able to track Romeg through his Internet IP address. Romeg was in Bastalayo and due to leave from a private airstrip. There wasn't much time, Sydney had to act quickly. He pulled out a set of car keys and then quietly eased out of his office, passing the room where Hernandez was sitting. He managed to get out of the building and to a car. After getting in the vehicle, he started it up and then drove off unnoticed. When he reached Delvo Boulevard, he picked up speed and headed toward the Cessna private airstrip. When he arrived, there was a blue Cadillac at one of the hangars. It had to be Romeg's. He got out of his car and headed toward the hangar.

AFTER DISCOVERING THE ambassador was gone, Hernandez checked the embassy and then realized one car was missing in the lot. She shouted to the secretary, "Who does that car that was in the stall belong to? Do you know where it is now?"

"It belongs to the ambassador. No, I don't know where it is," said the secretary.

"What is the license plate's number?"

The secretary hurried and gave Hernandez the information.

"Rollins, come in."

"What's up?"

"I need you to run this plate. Then trace the location of this car ASAP."

"It's at the Cessna private airstrip, west of the city."

Jumping in the green Hummer, she sped off in the direction of the airstrip, trying to reach Ed to advise of the situation, but was unable to make transmission. He must be in a dead zone, she thought. Trying again, this time to Seargent Sanchez, she got no response.

But Thornton heard the transmission, and chased after Hernandez, being about eleven miles away from her.

CHAPTER FORTY-EIGHT

Sydney entered the hangar door and saw Romeg waiting for him. "I'm not the same guy you beat in college," said Romeg.

"Doesn't matter who you think you are. I'm going to beat you down to the ground," said Sydney angrily.

Romeg pulled a small club from his pocket and swung it at Sydney's head. Sydney jumped back, barely getting out of the way, and he lunged at Romeg, blocking the club with his left arm while he grabbed him with his other one. After getting Romeg in a headlock, Sydney flung him over his side. Romeg slammed onto the ground, and Sydney quickly kicked him in his ribs. Romeg groaned in pain while trying to roll away and to avoid the second kick coming at him.

"Damn you! You killed Alicia, and you will pay for it now and for the rest of your life!" said Sydney.

"Kill her? No, you fool! I loved her. But I'm going to kill you for taking her from me."

Romeg jumped to his feet. He still had the club in his hand. Sydney attacked again, but Romeg moved faster this time, swiping across the jaw of Sydney with the club and stunning him. He then threw two right punches into Sydney's ribs. Sydney bent over from the blows, and Romeg brought the club smashing down on the backside of the ambassador's head. Sydney collapsed to the ground.

This time, it was Romeg looking over Sydney, and when he glanced over to his side, as Sydney had done to see Alicia's delight in their fistfight, he paused in shock. Alicia Benoit was standing there, and her eyes were wide open in excitement as she observed the battle and him. This time, he was the victor; he had finally taken his revenge.

Ah! But he was only hallucinating. When he looked again, his eyes saw who was actually in front of him. Alicia Benoit morphed and shimmered, and then Yolanda Hernandez was standing in her place.

"You had your fun, sonny. Now get ready for a real butt whippin'," she said.

Romeg charged toward Hernandez with the club poised to strike. He was very strong and moved quickly—but not quickly enough. Hernandez ran toward him, leaping into the air, thrusting both of her legs forward, and smashing into his chest. He fell back and crashed into a cement pillar, which he bounced off and hit a wall. Hernandez hit the ground and pounced back up to her feet. Romeg grabbed a metal chair that was beside him and hurled it at her. The specialist ducked, and the chair just missed her. She slid into Romeg's knees and jammed her boot into his thigh. Romeg, feeling the pain, went down, but he managed a solid punch to Hernandez's jaw, dazing her for a second.

"Damn it!" she said.

Both fighters got up from the ground, and Hernandez flung a reverse right-hand blow and knocked Romeg flat on his back. Romeg kicked at her, trying to make space between him and her. Grabbing a small table that was next to him, he swung it at her, catching her arm and shoulder.

"Oww!" she shouted. The blow had definitely hurt, but she was not about to give in to the pain.

Romeg swung the table again from the opposite side, catching Hernandez again. She thought, "This stops now." She rolled back away, getting out of the way of Romeg swinging the table. Jumping to her feet, she spotted the club Romeg had dropped during the fight. Picking it up, she looked over to Sydney, who was lying on the ground, still unable to get up; he was merely observing the battle with a dazed expression. Hernandez nodded to him and then turned back to Romeg, who was now charging her. She waited for him to come within striking distance; when he did, she leaped with her legs held open and caught him in a headlock with her strong thighs. With a powerful thrust, she twisted her body completely, flipping Romeg and smashing him to the ground. When he tried to recover, she bashed him in the forehead with the same club he had used on Sydney.

Romeg was knocked out cold. Hernandez looked over to Sydney and said, "Now that was a butt whippin'."

Sydney nodded in agreement.

SITTING IN THE small, but modern kitchen of his one bedroom suite, Clarence Dupont sipped on a glass of Hennessy. His thoughts were on his leaving Bastalayo. By the front door were two packed suitcases. The apartment furniture was all leased, everything else Dupont owned, he gave away to the local Christian charity center.

The sound of a honk, the cab he had ordered to take him to the airport. Clarence Dupont had resigned and was quietly leaving the American Island. Upon finishing the drink, he picked up both suitcases, walked out of the door and into the awaiting car. Looking back one last time, at his small abode, he then motioned to the driver to go. Knowing in the back of his mind, for his part in this ordeal, there would be a reckoning.

CHAPTER FOURTY-NINE

A black Explorer came speeding toward the small airstrip, where Romeg, Sydney, and Hernandez were. Its occupants were two gunmen, heavily armed with high-capacity assault rifles. One man was a tall, buff, heavyset man, and he had intense hazel eyes and wavy brown hair. The other man was not much smaller, and he was buff as well. Both men had a sense of lethality about them, appearing dreadful and deadly.

Rollins picked up a police scan that reported a car speeding in that direction, and using satellite surveillance with GPS tracking, he was able to detect the car and the weapons inside it. Then he radioed Thornton, who was about three miles behind the Explorer. Putting two and two together, Thornton chased the vehicle, frantically trying to radio ahead.

"Hernandez, this is Thornton. Come on, Yolie, answer! Come in, damn it!" he said, shouting into his radio. He was grasping the jeep's steering wheel so tightly that his right hand looked as white as snow, and his left hand was clamping down the button on his radio. "Come in, Yolie! Do you hear me? You've got two assailants coming your way quickly, and they're armed and deadly." Extremely frustrated, his adrenaline pumping sky high, Thornton threw the radio to the seat next to him, and he tried to ram the gas pedal through the jeep's baseboard. "Crap! Yolanda, you better be ready for these guys!" he said to himself.

The SUV raced into the almost-empty parking lot, and the driver slammed his foot on the brakes, bringing the truck to a screeching stop right beside Hernandez's Hummer. Her radio had been damaged during the fight with Romeg, and her 9 mm was lying on the ground too far away from her when the two men entered the hangar. She saw the men point their weapons in her direction, and without hesitation, she jumped behind a large, metal pole that supported the roof of the hangar, but not before a bullet hit her. It went into her side, right above the waist. She grunted while holding her side where the bullet had entered and then looked around for something that could help her fight back. There was nothing. The smaller man fired repeatedly at both sides of the beam, while slowly approaching her. She would have to jump out and rush the shooter; most likely, she would take another bullet in the attempt to overtake him.

"This is not going to end well," she thought.

Across the floor was Sydney. He had regained some of his wits, but he remained lying on the ground and pretending to be dead, peeping to see if there was anything he could do. There was no weapon near him either, so any attempt to attack the assailants would be suicide for him. Feeling hopeless, he lay there, praying for an opportunity. If he had to die, he would do so trying something. He would not let Hernandez go out like that.

He was about to try to get up when the larger assailant, seeing Romeg lying unconscious, ran over to Romeg and picked him up like a sack of potatoes and threw him over his shoulders; then he signaled to his partner to get out of there quickly. The large man scurried out of the hangar with his partner, backing out and firing spurts of bullets toward the pole that Hernandez was hiding behind. The men raced back to their Explorer, and the smaller man stopped and sprayed the Hummer's tires with bullets. They hopped in their vehicle and sped to the end to the airstrip, where Romeg's private plane sat idling. Another man, presumably the pilot, was waiting inside, and after the two men boarded (the larger one carrying Romeg's unconscious body), the plane hurried down the runway; within minutes, it was in the air. Thornton saw the Cessna fly away to the northeast.

Thornton jumped out his jeep and ran into the empty hangar. Hernandez and Sydney were now trying to help one another. Both were badly hurt: Hernandez was bleeding profusely, and Sydney had a huge knot on the back of his head.

"I couldn't get you on your radio. Man, Yolie, you're bleeding. Let me see."

Moving her hand away from the wound, Thornton ripped a sleeve off his shirt and stuffed it over the wound and put Hernandez's hand back on it. Meanwhile, the ambassador was getting dizzy and almost fell.

"Keep the pressure on it, Yolie. What happened to him?"

"Romeg smashed him in the head with a club; he might have a concussion. Boy, that was close. They were Romeg's men for sure. They stopped firing and grabbed him and then hightailed it out of here. I must have broken my radio in the fight with Romeg."

After inspecting the lump on the ambassador's head, Thornton became certain the ambassador was in bad shape. Thornton's only thoughts were to get them both medical care. A deep look of worry crossed Thornton's face when viewed Hernandez's wound a second time.

"I saw them fly away in a plane," said Thornton. "Right now, I don't give a darn about them—I need to get you both to a hospital."

"Wow, Thornton, don't get so worried—you're not getting rid of me that easy," said Hernandez. "Is that the look your dad had when you accidently shot that shotgun off?"

Thornton caught Hernandez's meaning and realized he was falling for her. "You're darn right I'm not losing you to this. Where else will I get such a badass partner like you?"

Thornton, supporting Hernandez and the ambassador, helped them walk outside to the parking lot. Hernandez looked at the bullet-riddled tires on her hummer. "Looks like we're riding with you, Thornton."

"How many bad guys are we fighting here? I count five, possibly seven, so far. Makes me wonder how deep this guy's connections are. I think Uncle Sam should give us a raise," said Thornton.

"Yeah, right," said Hernandez, "like that's gonna happen. Anyway, you know you love the action, just as much as I do."

"If I can get some of it. So far, you're the one getting all the butt-kicking action."

"No worries. I'm sure there is more on the way."

Thornton radioed Sergeant Miller, who was following up a hunch about Jay Snyder, Evelyn Thomas's chauffer, with Williams and Kaboo. Thornton filled him in with the details about the event. Ed looked at Marrio, who was there with him. "I need you to meet them at the hospital and watch over the ambassador," said Ed. "I'll handle this."

Both men made fists then punched each other's knuckles lightly. Ed radioed Rollins and the new man and told them to stay alert while they watched over the girls at the ambassador's home, which Rollins and the new guy already had on lockdown.

CHAPTER FIFTY

E d's cell phone rang; Detective Wilson Williams was calling. Detective Kaboo was driving. "Miller, meet me at the gas station on Seaboard Street and Crane Road. It's in North Town. I'll pick you up there," said Williams. When they met up, both Williams and Kaboo were in the car. "Jump in" said Williams? "Where the back seat? You taking me to jail?" Ed said, being humerous. Williams looked at Ed and responded. Sorry man these cars don't have that much room in the front." The three-exchanged information, putting the pieces together, while Williams drove to an area that was mostly four story apartment buildings.

Detective Le Kwok, back at the precinct, had discovered information about the fictitious Jay Snyder, whose name they now knew to be Floyd Rochester and had given the info to Williams, who was now following it up. The car came to a stop. Looking back at Miller, who was in the rear seat of the undercover police car, Williams said, "You will need to stay in the car because this is local police business. Detective Kaboo and I will handle this."

"Sure, Wilson. I'll just be right here when you get back," said Ed.

The address Le Kwok had given them ended up taking them to a four-story apartment building made of brownstone. Looking around, Williams saw cars parked along the side street; scanning further, he saw some that were very nice. The two detectives got out of their dark-brown Impala SS and walked toward the entrance of the building.

Ed looked up and spotted someone peeping out of a window on the third floor. He watched the detectives disappear into the large glass doors of the building. However, he could not sit still: his gut feeling sensed something was off, so he got out of the car and went around to the back of the apartment complex. After going through a small alley and passing some trash cans and an old dumpster with graffiti on it, Ed spotted the man from the photo, Floyd Rochester, coming out of the rear door.

Rochester spotted Ed and then started to run. Ed chased him, and they ran across the street, one block over from where Williams's car was parked. Rochester fled down an alley, and Ed continued his hot pursuit, staying about three hundred feet behind the man. Rochester raced through the door of another brownstone apartment building and headed up some stairs to the roof. Ed picked up the pace, clearing three steps at a time, closing the gap between him and the man.

It dawned on Ed that this man probably knew the area well.

After reaching the rooftop, Ed looked around and saw Rochester leap across a gap between the building they were on and the next one. The man, sailing forward, fell about fifteen feet and then landed and rolled on the next building's rooftop. The next gap between buildings was about twenty feet wide. Rochester cleared that space as well, landed on that building's flat tar-mat roof, and rolled again in one fluid motion. And he kept going, heading for the next building.

Ed stopped briefly at the first jump, evaluating the distance, which allowed Floyd time to gain more distance.

"Well, I'm glad I've been running," thought Ed. He drew back, sprinted, and made the leap. On each consecutive building, he picked up speed, timing his leaps and rolls perfectly.

By the time, Ed caught up to Rochester, the man had run through the roof's door and had locked it behind him. Ed yanked at the door and tried to kick it down, but the door remained unforgiving. He looked around for another way down, spotted a fire escape on the north side of the roof, and ran toward it. Moving speedily down the fire escape, Ed was thinking ahead; he figured that Rochester would not head back in the direction of where the detectives' car was parked, but Rochester probably owned one of those cars alongside the apartment complex. Ed wondered whether the man would try to get to his vehicle from the opposite side of the building.

It was worth a shot to see.

Ed headed back in that direction. He remembered that one of the cars was a new, pristine sedan—one that a chauffeur might have. Ed tried calling Williams to give him a heads-up, believing the detectives could get there sooner. The call went straight to Williams's voice mail.

"Come on Wilson—get off the phone!" said Ed.

Ed ran at full speed to get back. There, his guess turned out to be right: as he reached the corner where the sedan was, he saw that Rochester was walking quickly toward it, trying to act casual to avoid drawing any attention, but when he saw Ed, he then made a beeline for the car. After getting into it, he pushed the start button on the dash and tried to throw it into drive, but Ed grabbed the door handle of the driver's side and yanked it open before Rochester could accelerate. After grabbing him by his collar, Ed jerk him hard once, pulling him out of the car and to the ground.

Floyd tried to fight, but one quick punch from Ed terminated his effort.

Williams and Kaboo came around the corner just as the altercation was over. They looked at Ed.

"I thought I told you to stay in the car," said Williams.

"You did, but after you went in, I saw this guy peeping out the window and didn't think he was going to wait around to have a pleasant chat with you."

Meanwhile, Detective Kaboo was handcuffing the man and reading him his rights.

"Thank you and nice work, soldier," said Williams. "We'll get this guy down to the precinct and see what he knows."

"You're welcome. And I'll try to stay in the car next time."

"Next time? You mean we are going to do this again?"

"Who knows, Wilson? You are growing on me, so maybe I'll stick around."

Later, a patrol car pulled up, and Detective Kaboo tucked Rochester into the back seat and then went back to Williams and Ed. All three of them got into the dark-brown Impala SS and headed back to the gas station, where Ed's steel-gray Challenger was parked.

CHAPTER FIFTY-ONE

A Call from Franco

Everything, once again, settled down for the time being. Hernandez was recovering from her gunshot wound and was released from the hospital. The ambassador had to take it easy for a few weeks after sustaining a mild concussion from his fight with Romeg, who had managed to flee the island and out of US jurisdiction. The Government's best guess, he was held up in Venezuela or Africa, but Ed was unsure because of all the misinformation out there. In any event, the matter would be handled later. However, with things being somewhat normal again, the team could step back and take a breath.

Ed's phone rang, and he saw that Franco De Angelo, who was one of Ed's closest friends, was calling. Franco was married to Ed's cousin Charee, who was the daughter of his father's brother. Ed, Franco, and Charee had grown up together in Philadelphia. Franco and Charee fell in love when he and Ed were in high school. Up to that point, Ed felt that she would always be his little cousin, but suddenly she grew up. Franco tried to keep from falling for her, and Ed believed that Franco's resistance came from his not wanting to anger Ed. As it turned out, Ed had thought the situation quite humorous; he had already recognized Franco and Charee's connection, and he did not have a problem with their being together. What was important to Ed was that Franco should treat her right. Charee was two years younger than Ed, and he thought of her as a sister. Both Franco and Charee ended up going to college together in Los Angeles, and later they went to law school together. Franco became a successful prosecutor, and Charee became a successful entertainment lawyer.

"Hey, Franco," said Ed. "It's been a while. How are you doing?"

"Great! Things are going really well for us."

"I'm glad to hear it, and I heard you're moving up on your job."

"Yeah, I'm not too far from the top of the food chain. What's happening with you?"

"Just the normal shoot-'em-up drama—running down the bad guys, protecting the people."

"Yeah, well, be careful out there. By the way, I wanted to tell you that Rosie is having another baby. We're flying back to Philly to see the family. We'll probably stop off and see your uncle and mom," said Franco. Rosie was Franco's baby sister.

"Oh wow! Tell them congratulations for me." Ed paused for a moment, enjoying thoughts of family, but then another thought came to his mind. He asked, "Whatever happened to the case you and the district attorney were working on? The one with the mob dude."

"That case! It's a hell of a mess. You know my father is high up in the local mafia, but the defendant is part of the LA mob, who is putting pressure on my father to talk me out of pursuing a conviction. You know I can't do that. I'm not built that way, and my father, though I know the situation is stressing him, won't bow down before any coercion."

"So you're going to take this guy down?"

"Yeah, as far as I'm concerned, he's going down."

The two friends continued their conversation for about an hour. After all the catching up was done, they said their good-byes and hung up.

CHAPTER FIFTY-TWO

It was Wednesday night, and Ed decided to mix up the shifts. Tonight, he would free up most of the team. He and Thornton would take the night shift, and the team would be free until noon on Thursday.

Marrio had spent all of his free time with Crystal during the four-plus months he had been in Bastalayo, and their connection had become very strong. The unusual thing for Marrio was the fact that Crystal had never slept with a man. Marrio was accustomed to intimate relations, but Crystal was special, so he was okay with it. Whenever he was off duty, he could think only about seeing her. Marrio had not told her that he would be off that night when Ed mixed up the shifts, because he wanted to surprise her. Upon leaving the base, he went out to Hell Fighter, and stretching his leg across her smooth black leather seat, he felt its firm and perfect fit. His hands firmly gripped the handle bars, and he got the feeling of being one with the bike.

No one was paying attention when the news reported that the sun had expelled a burst of energy, which was making its way to the earth. It had occurred on Sunday, three days ago, and would take a total of three days to reach the planet. Wednesday was the third day, and it had arrived. What would happen is the cloud burst would move across the planet's atmosphere, affecting earth's magnetic fields on the North and South Poles, causing strange events, along with displaying a most amazing picture in the sky. It was called the aurora borealis, also known as the northern lights. This was not uncommon by itself, but every now and then, what would happen is the magnetic effects of the northern lights would meet up with those of the aurora australis, or the southern lights, and the meet up would happen right around the Caribbean, where Bastalayo lay, right next to the Bermuda Triangle. This meeting of the northern and southern lights—along with it being the time of year when the earth was closest to the sun and when the moon was closest to the earth—would cause strange and mystical events.

Marrio reached for his cell phone and dialed Crystal's digits. He waited for her to answer.

"Hi, Marrio," she said.

Her voice came softly and sensually across his cell, and he was momentarily taken aback—her voice was penetrating deep into his psyche and splashing into his mind, body, and soul. He could feel his will and emotions surrendering to her voice. He said, "Hi, Crystal. What are you doing?"

She gave a mild moan. "I was thinking," she said.

"Thinking? Thinking about what?"

"Oh, thinking about how nice it would be if you were here with me."

Marrio had not told her that she was about to get her wish, but before he did, he wanted to enjoy the mood she was in. "Oh, babe, I really want to be with you too," he said.

"Couldn't you take the night off and come to me?" she asked, again speaking softly and sensually.

Marrio's body pulsated with pleasure at the sound of her sweet voice, and reciprocated her tone with his own soft and deep tone. "Babe, you know I want to be there with you. If I was there right now, I would have you in my arms, and I wouldn't stop kissing you until the sun came up," he said.

"Oh, honey, that's sounds so good."

Marrio's mind was racing; they had not shared this kind of intimate talk before, which was challenging his willpower. Marrio felt something special for Crystal: the fact she was a virgin intrigued him, and he was determined to stay respectful and not force her past her boundaries. She had told him that she was saving herself for the one person she believed would be her soul mate.

Right then, though, his body was making a strong statement, voicing its own desires, and it would take everything in Marrio to stop his urges. It was not helping that she was sounding so welcoming over the phone. Marrio felt as if he were tasting her words as they left her mouth. He squirmed on Hell Fighter, trying to adjust from the sensation he felt from the sudden swelling between his thighs. He needed space to ease the pain from the awkward position of his manhood.

"Wow!" he thought. "This is a serious switch in roles. She is the seducer, and I'm being seduced."

He had all that he could take, but he wanted more. After firing up Hell Fighter, he could still hear Crystal through his bluetooth headpiece, which was a special military design that could suppress all outside noise to a near-zero level. Even Hell Fighter's ferocious engine could not overwhelm the device, only what was spoken directly into the microphone, which was positioned in front of Marrio's mouth.

He left, speeding in the direction of Crystal's home, and he decided to toy a little with her emotions. He would stimulate her mentally by thrusting all the affection he could at her—he would go back to being the seducer and she the prey. The boundary had been breached. As Hell Fighter roared, so did Marrio on the inside.

Crystal lay across her bed, wearing a silk night gown that was dark blue and embossed with sky-blue lace. While lying upon her side with her phone in one hand, she slid her other fingers down the tower of her neck, between her breasts, and along her stomach. Her fingers then came to rest at the edge of her untouched garden. She slowly slid her left foot gently up the side of her right leg, rubbing her manicured toes against the back of her calf.

Neither she nor Marrio could control the wonderful madness that had overcome them. As Marrio approached her home, he slowed down and parked Hell Fighter beyond the fence at the rear of the house's backyard. Then he turned off the powerful engine of the motorcycle. He was out of sight.

They continued the conversation a bit longer, uttering to each other whatever sweet things popped into their heads, but then she heard the doorbell ring. Crystal wondered who could be ringing her doorbell at that time of night unannounced. Looking through the peephole on the door, she saw Marrio. She quickly tossed the phone onto her brown couch, which was to her right and in front of a large Anderson-style window that covered most of the wall. She then hastily opened the door. He could hardly enter before she leaped onto him, wrapping her arms around his neck and her legs around his waist.

"Oh God! How did you pull this off, you slickster?" she asked, all the time kissing his face. "I thought you were working tonight?"

Marrio smelled the freshness of her body, along with the sweet lotion she was wearing. She felt soft and firm at the same time. "I wanted to surprise you; I wanted tonight to be special," he said.

"Well, you made it special," she answered, still embracing him.

Feeling her this way, as she rubbed against him with her silk night gown, in her home, on this crazy night, he could do nothing but absorb the intoxication of the moment. His senses took in every bit of this woman in his arms; everything in him screamed, "I want you!"

Crystal ran her hands through his hair and slowly down to his chest and then back up his neck and to his cheeks, where they came to rest. She drew closer for a long, slow, wet kiss. Her sultry brown eyes locked on his, and the tiger-eyed warrior looked back. As their mouths joined, he pulled her in tightly, gripping her buttocks and carrying her through the bedroom and to a door that led to the back yard.

"Where are you taking me?" she asked in a low tone, breathing heavily from the passion coursing through her. She moaned at the strength in his arms, at how powerfully he held her.

When they were outside, Marrio looked up and whispered to Crystal, telling her to look up as well. She no longer questioned why he had taken her outside. Gazing into the sky, she saw the magnificent northern lights as they came together with the southern lights. It was awe inspiring. He stood her up. After mounting on Hell Fighter in a backward position, he beckoned Crystal to climb on, which she did.

She allowed herself the pleasure of exploring Marrio, feeling the strength in his arms and the hardness of his body; then she wandered lower until she reached his manly parts and discovered he was well endowed. Marrio took the privilege of exploring her as well, and when his hand slowly went up under her gown, he found her soft, warm, and moist. Crystal groaned and gently bit Marrio's lip as his hand brushed over her garden. The two became absorbed in the heated moment, and Marrio tried everything in his power to pull back, but could not. Crystal submerged her soft, wet tongue deep into Marrio's mouth, smothering him in a wave of passion. After staggering his mind with her kiss, she withdrew her lips from his and said, "I'm ready."

CHAPTER FIFTY-THREE

Detective Williams stood in his office, holding a cup of coffee, while gazing out his office window. It had been a week since they had brought Floyd Rochester in for questioning. They did not have enough proof to hold him for intent of murder; all they had was a man who used a fictitious name to claim a car from a salvage yard. In the investigation of Alicia's death, the state had ruled out murder, and even though Williams had a theory of what might have happened, he still did not have the car, which he could examine to prove his theory true or false. Also, he needed to establish a motive. Floyd Rochester's explanation for getting Alicia Ballantyne's totaled Tesla was that he could have sold it for a profit. He said that he had wanted to sell it to an anonymous collector who bought items that had stories of intrigue and drama behind them—such as a story of an important socialite dying in a horrible car accident.

The state prosecutor was insistent on not reopening the case, being that it was an election year. Along with that, the ambassador was still somewhat in denial. When the accident first happened, he and the girls had gone through so much during their time of mourning, and he did not want his daughters to relive that terrible time, seeing as they had moved on.

Just then, Detective Kaboo walked in. "What's on your mind, Wilson?"

"I'm just going over in my head what we know about Floyd Rochester. That guy gets the Tesla out of the salvage yard and supposedly sells it to a collector that buys cars with stories behind them. Where did Rochester get the money to buy it? And how convenient that this collector is from Venezuela, which is out of our reach, along with the car. I get that the ambassador didn't want to face dealing with the wrecked Tesla, but he bought too quickly into Alicia's death being an accident; he simply collected the insurance money and expressed no further concerns about the remains of the car. And the salvage yard had a legal right to dispose of the car in any way it deemed suitable."

"Umm, so let's say that is the case. Why did Rochester run? Why would Evelyn Thomas bail him out of jail and provide an attorney for him?"

"Yeah, she was Johnny-on-the-spot with the lawyer. Maybe there's something going on between those two," said Williams.

"How about this: we know that Romeg Thomas was obsessed with Alicia Ballantyne, so much so that he was ready to kill out of jealousy. Perhaps Evelyn, his wife, was jealous Romeg's feelings for Alicia, so Evelyn decided to remove the competition, meaning Alicia Ballantyne. After all, Evelyn supposedly loved Romeg all her life, and I can only imagine being in love with a man whose heart was ensnared by another woman. And let's say, for argument's sake, that she paid off Rochester to rig the car to fail."

"Or maybe she didn't pay him off with cash but suckered him with love or sex. She is a beautiful and powerful woman, so she could have easily enthralled this Floyd Rochester. I could see him doing whatever it took to stay in her life."

"You know we're stretching it!" said Kaboo.

"Yeah but the pieces fit. If only we could get that car."

The detectives gazed out the window, pondering the implications of their suppositions.

CHAPTER FIFTY-FOUR

I t was a Saturday morning, about five months into the assignment. Ed pulled the steel-gray Challenger up to Lucius Sucoy's
beach home. He climbed out of the driver's seat and walked up
to the front door. After ringing the doorbell, he heard Lucius say,
"Come in. The door is open."

Ed walked in. He was wearing black flip-flops, an army T-shirt
that revealed his six-pack abs, and an orange and blue bathing
suit, which fit tightly around his thighs and almost stretched down
to his knees. Sharks and whales were imprinted on the suit.

"Is Angelina ready?" he asked.

"She has already gone down to the water and said you should
meet her down there," said Lucius. "Go left and down to the
Blowhole—it's about a quarter of a mile down the beach."

Ed took off running in a light jog. When he arrived, he simply
stopped and took in the view. The Blowhole was amazing: a variety of tropical trees, both small and large, were scattered about the
area, interspersed with several ocean bushes. Wildlife moved within
it as well. Seagulls were sitting on the rocks, and several sea turtles

were lying lazily in the sand. Not far from them was a group of rocks in the form of stepping stones, which led into the cave known as the Blowhole. The water itself was baby blue and crystal clear, and at its bottom sat red coral, next to the plush underwater plants. There were blue tangs and clown fish playing in the corner of the cave.

Angelina broke through the surface of the water, scattering water droplets through the air, which shimmered like diamonds. Her long, dark hair lay behind her, and water dripped off her face. Her beautiful brown eyes glistened, and when she smiled, the whole cave seemed to light up with a new illumination, brightening everything—or so it seemed to Ed. She rhythmically bounced in the water, creating little waves that traveled outward and lulled Ed into a somewhat dreamy feeling. "Wow," he thought, "every time I see this woman, she mesmerizes me."

"Are you going to just stand there, or are you coming in?"

"Snapping out of it, Ed shouted, "Yeah! heck yeah! You don't have to tell me twice."

Plunging in, he swam toward her, diving under the water and resurfacing behind her. After putting his arms around her, he spoke into her ear: "My God! You are so beautiful—how did I get so lucky?"

She brushed her cheek against the side of his. "I can say the same. We are both so lucky. Kiss me."

He turned her around so that she would face him, and their bodies pressed together. She wrapped her arms around his neck as he wrapped his around her waist. For an eternity, they stayed locked in a kiss. When they finally released, Angelina tilted her head and laid it between his neck and shoulders. Ed became fond of how she would rest her head there. It made him feel so special and important to her. As they stood clinging to each other in the water, he thought, "There is nothing I wouldn't do for this woman." He felt his heart plunge into a deeper level of emotion—where he felt a mild fear: it dawned on him that he had fallen deeply in love.

After embracing and showering each other with affection, they swam down into the deeper part of the ocean, exploring the magnificent beauty of the sea. Ed felt amazement at seeing this new world of underwater life. In some of his past missions, he deep-sea dived off the coast of Africa, but those waters did not have even half the beauty of this paradise.

Ed and Angelina held hands, swimming down deep into the sea, pointing to the different wonders they sighted, feeling so connected and oblivious to everything else in the world. They were in the moment, in bliss, and in love.

When they had finished exploring, they walked out of the sea and lay on the sandy beach, not far from where they had started. There was a cool breeze blowing upon Ed's chest. Holding her in his arms, her hair gently blowing in the wind, Ed knew this was the one, his gift from God. He was thankful, and he was humble. Angelina looked over Ed's gorgeous body and noticed a scar. Running the tip of her fingers over it, she asked, "What happened here?"

"War wound. I really don't talk about it."

Pressing the subject, she asked another question, being very compassionate in her tone: "Is it painful? I don't mean the wound, but the memory."

He had not been this close to a woman before—he had not let them know his pain, but he wanted to let Angelina in. He felt vulnerable but trusted her.

"I was in Afghanistan on a special mission that occurred during a very bad time there. The war had escalated, and our troops were having a rough go at it. My team was deep in a suspected Al-Qaeda area, and we were to get intelligence info from an inside spy. Even though I was a seasoned soldier, the stress and pressures were almost overwhelming. We didn't think we would make it home that time. Within seconds, any one of us could die from a sniper's bullet, a land mine, or a rocket. There was no one I could really trust outside of my team. On one particular night of the mission, I lay down to get some rest. It was hot, over one hundred degrees, and the area was dusty. My mouth was dry, and my body was sweaty."

Ed stopped smiling before he continued. "Good thing I had trained in the deserts of Arizona. 'It's just like being back in the old office,' said Bobby Bradford, one of my teammates. He was a good kid and hell of a soldier. He was from Oakland, California. I remember him lying beside me and sweating like a pig in a furnace and cussing like a sailor. I told him, 'Man this is the army, not the navy,' but he just looked at me and spurted off a few more choice words. We had been lodged within that cave for two weeks, waiting to make contact."

Ed stopped again briefly and looked into her deep, cutting eyes. He allowed himself to take in more of her beautiful, slender body and its olive-brown complexion and her long, lovely legs. As they rested on the warm and sandy beach, he thought, "She truly is a work of art. She is so perfect. Perhaps love is blind—who knows?" Ed was trained to notice details, and he certainly did not miss any of hers.

He continued his story. "The night edged on, and sometime in the early morning hours, gunshots rang through the cave. I could hear Cory Engleton, another one of my teammates, yell, 'Uggghh, I'm hit!' More shots rang out, ricocheting off the walls of the cave. I heard another scream coming from another comrade, Carlos; he was hit in the shoulder. He yelled out, 'I'm all right—see about Cory!' Cory had taken one in the neck and was pinned down behind a large rock. We couldn't get to him. By this time, our whole team was in full operation."

Ed was now fully engaged in remembering all the details. He spoke almost hypnotically, the memories flowing and taking him back.

"I yelled out at the top of my lungs, 'Ambush front, ambush front! Blue team, counter the ambush, right flank! Gold team, suppressive fire! Give 'em hell!'

"We moved into action quickly. Devon Davis, another soldier on my team, caught sight of where one sniper was and quickly did some sniping of his own. He took that guy out in one shot. His killing the enemy sniper opened up an exit for us. We were able to get out of the cave and gain fair angles against the enemy. We were better trained than they were, and we had the most modern weapons.

"The whole fight lasted fifteen minutes, and then it was over. The team did well, but when I looked around, I didn't see Bobby; everyone was accounted for, except him. We had taken out four of the enemy at the cost of both Carlos and Cory being wounded. When we went to where Bobby was, he was lying still and quiet—no longer cussing, no longer sweating, no longer with us. No one had died on my watch before. It was surreal. During all the drama and adrenaline, I had not noticed that I had caught a bullet and was losing a considerable amount of blood. I remember falling on my back, being faint from the loss of blood; I looked up at Devon Davis, and told him, 'Handle it, man.' I woke up three days later in a hospital bed. They had flown me back to Walter Reed Hospital, where I recovered. And that's it, the whole story."

"And what about Marrio, was he there?"

"No, not on that mission. At the time, he was on a reconnaissance mission, east of us, about 150 miles away."

Angelina brushed her fingers again over the scar. Bending over, she kissed it; then she held his face in her hands and kissed him deeply and slowly. After pulling back, she laid her head on his shoulder. Ed exhaled and rested his head upon hers.

CHAPTER FIFTY-FIVE

An ocean liner pulled up to the docks in Cuba. Three men were standing by the side of the rails and peering downward in search of their contact. A tall, thin Cuban man stared back and waved toward the men, signaling he was the one. The ship's giant horn blew loudly one final time before the ship came to a stop. With the passengers now departing the boat, Romeg Thomas told one of his associates to handle the luggage, and he and the other man went to meet the Cuban waiting at the bottom of the ramp. The Cuban extended his hand, as did Romeg.

"It's good to see you again," said the Cuban.

"Yes, it's been a while."

"Was your trip well?"

"It was. No incidents. Is everything ready?" asked Romeg.

"Yes," said the Cuban, "we have everything you asked for. We made accommodations for you under the name of Louis Bel-Fontaine. No one will know you are here." He handed Romeg a package. "Here is your new identification. You will find that everything is in order."

"And what about transportation?"

"Yes, we have procured a slightly used BMW, which should help you keep a low profile. Your driver will be Tomaso; he is one of my best men and knows the lay of the land."

"One more thing," said Romeg, "I want comfort tonight. You do remember what I like?"

The Cuban was well aware of Romeg's sexual preferences and had anticipated that this would be one of his requests. Romeg always wanted a young woman who was petite, clever, and fiery— that is, someone who resembled his lost love, Alicia Ballantyne. He would have these women dress in particular clothing that Alicia used to wear, and he would have them read from a script he had written to suit his exotic fantasies. It was always the same fantasy, but the script played out in various ways, the roles shifting to suit new versions of Romeg's lost love. It was no wonder that Evelyn could never overcome the ghost of Alicia Ballantyne.

"Yes, we have addressed the needs of your particular tastes."

"Very well, I will contact you if there is anything else I need," said Romeg.

The Cuban man walked away, and Romeg and his assistants were now heading for the BMW, where Tomaso was already waiting. The one man with Romeg was named Myron, and he was his number one man and personal bodyguard, and he also handled all of Romeg's dirty work. He was the one who had carried Romeg during the rescue at the private airstrip. The other man was Jorge, who was Myron's sidekick. The four men got into the car.

Romeg said, "Looks like we will be staying low for a while, so get comfortable, men." And the car drove off.

CHAPTER FIFTY-SIX

Floyd Rochester, after released from jail, sat down on the red and black couch that was in his living room. He pulled his cell phone out and called Evelyn Thomas. He was a little hesitant at dialing her number, not wanting to get her angry or suffer her rebuke, knowing he would have to tell her everything he had told the police. Even though he had covered his story well, he knew she would still drill him. He did not like upsetting her; anything that might take him out of her grace worried him. He could hear the ringing on his phone, and then she answered.

"Hello, are you alone?" said Floyd.

"Yes, what is it?"

"I need to tell you how the police pulled me in, and questioned me about the car."

"The Tesla? What did you tell them?"

"Nothing that could hurt us. Just what we had gone over."

Evelyn Thomas was a very thorough person; and leaving nothing to chance, she continued to drill Floyd. "Whom did you talk with?"

"Detective Williams and Detective Kaboo, a lady cop. They came to my apartment to get me. I ran, and they hunted me down."

"Why in the hell did you do that?" asked Evelyn, becoming angry. "That makes you look guilty of something."

"I'm sorry. I panicked and ran. It wasn't even the detectives who caught me. It was Sergeant Miller, some military guy. I don't know how he's involved."

"It doesn't matter. They are on to us, but are you sure they can't trace the car?"

Floyd thought for a moment. "I'm pretty sure," he said.

"Pretty sure? That is not good enough—you better be darn sure. We could go to jail for a long time. As long as they don't have the car, there is little they can do. I want you to double-check with that buyer and make sure that car never surfaces. But before you do that, come over here. I don't want to be alone tonight."

Floyd was excited to hear this. She was his whole world, even with the danger and drama, and life without her would be boring. Floyd smiled and nodded his head to himself and then said, "I'll be there."

CHAPTER FIFTY-SEVEN

The next day had come, and after the beautiful time Ed had with Angelina, he was seeing life in a whole new way. Marrio, Rollins, and Thornton were going over some plans for the ambassador's schedule when Ed walked in.

"Good morning," said Marrio.

"Great morning and a great weekend—now I'm ready to rock and roll. I take it that is the ambassador's schedule you guys are working on," said Ed.

"Yeah, it is," said Marrio. "The ambassador, in spite of what has happened, is doing all right. He's got a full agenda today and seems quite chipper—just as you appear to be," said Marrio, winking.

Thornton looked a second time at Ed and smiled, then lowered his head back to his work.

Marrio drew me to the side, into the main living room, and he said, "So tell me what is going on. You've got this glowy thing about you."

Ed looked at Marrio. Ed trusted him with deeper personal matters, so he opened up. "I think I'm in love with Angelina; as a matter of fact, I *know* I'm in love with her."

"Okay, I can relate, man. So what now?" said Marrio, reflecting on the fact that he was in love with Crystal.

"I can't settle down: my life is the army. I'm always seeing new adventures, dangers, and new challenges, so I got to keep moving."

"I feel you," said Marrio. "It's funny how you and I are so much alike in that area."

"Yeah! So I take it you are facing the same dilemma too—having to choose your career or love. You know how Angelina's life is here on Bastalayo; I'm not ready for that."

"Me neither, but I don't want to lose Crystal. I've never been moved by another woman the way Crystal makes me feel."

"So, are you saying you're going to stay here? Our mission is up at the end of the month," said Ed.

"Hell! I don't know; I'm as confused about this as you are. My spirit was free, but all of a sudden, my heart is captured, and my mind is almost ready to give in. I'd like to spend more time before deciding, but Bastalayo is so far from home. I need to get back to San Antonio, so I can think this all over."

Ed was struck by a funny thought, and he laughed. "I thought we were talking about me. Seeing as we are both in the same boat, maybe we could get them to enlist; then we could take them with us."

Marrio joined in the humor. "Then we'd have to train them. You know that's not happening," he said.

Both men walked over to the window of the main room.

Marrio said, "Nothing would please my parents more than to see me settle down with a wife and take over the ranch."

"We'd better get to work," said Ed. "We need to get everything in order for the next team."

Ed's phone rang; Kwame was calling. Ed ended his conversation with Marrio and switched his attention to the phone call with Kwame.

"What's up Kwame?" said Ed.

"I've got some crazy news for you about Alicia Ballantyne's car."

Ed paused for a second, giving his mind time to switch gears. "All right, I'm listening."

"I had some power players from Venezuela come to my club. They had a few drinks and were borderline drunk. I stopped at their table to welcome them to my club, and we chatted for a while. One of them was surfing the news on his cell phone, and he came across last week's story about Romeg Thomas. He said he knew him and his wife, Evelyn. I gave them a complimentary bottle of Dom Perignon, and in gratitude, they relaxed and talked loosely, including the guy who knows Romeg Thomas and Evelyn. I found out that the guy has season soccer tickets next to the man that purchased Mrs. Ballantyne's Tesla."

Ed was floored by the information he was hearing. "What a stroke of luck!" he thought.

"Tell me you have a name," said Ed.

"I can do better. The man's name is Lawrence Trotman III, and he lives in Venezuela. But here's the bonus—you got a pen and paper ready?"

Ed quickly walked over to a table and retrieved a pen and paper. "Go ahead. I'm ready."

Kwame spat out some digits. "That's his phone number," he said.

"Kwame, you are off the charts! I owe you big."

"No, man! You don't owe me anything; I'm just glad to be able to help." Kwame then changed the subject. "So, when are you leaving?"

"End of the month. I will be heading to the big AZ - Valley of the Sun."

"The Valley of the Sun? Where is that?" asked Kwame.

"Phoenix, Arizona! You know, like Cali' or the Big Apple. Phoenix has a nickname too."

"Okay, I've got to remember that. So, what about the girl?"

Ed paused not ready with an answer, so he responded to Kwame's question differently. "I'll see her this weekend, and she and I will talk."

Kwame picked up mixed signals from Ed's words and tone. Through his phone, Ed heard someone talk to Kwame. It was one of his bartenders.

"Mr. Taylor, we need you up front; the inspector is here," said the bartender.

"Crap! I'm sorry, Ed, but I've got to see this food inspector and make sure all my ducks are in a row. Look, come down when you get time. I'd like to see you before you leave."

"Sure thing, Kwame. Thanks again for everything."

"No problem."

CHAPTER FIFTY-EIGHT

Lucius Sucoy was sitting in his kitchen and looking out a window that faced the beach. He watched the ocean's waves swell and crash and dissolve.

"Good morning, Grandpa," said a voice coming from the kitchen door.

"Not turning around, he replied, "Good morning, my sweet baby girl."

Angelina came up behind him and kissed him upon his head. "Umm, that coffee smells good; I think I'll join you with a cup," she said.

"Please do, and tell me about how things are with you," said Lucius.

"Things are good, and I couldn't be happier. I am up for a promotion at the hospital; I am about to become an assistant director in the cancer ward—something I've been working very hard for."

"Ah yes, you always had a passion to help cancer patients," replied Lucius. He did not say it, but he knew the root of it started when her grandmother died of leukemia. Angelina watched her slowly wither away and felt helpless at the time. This happened back when she had finished college. When she would visit her grand-mother at the hospital, she would stop in other patients' rooms and try to comfort them and their loved ones as well. Angelina was a tall and slender girl, and like her mother, she was astonishingly beautiful, almost to a point beyond belief. She was very intelligent, quick, and witty and excelled in education.

When Angelina finished high school, her father sent her to college. He believed education was the essential path to success, so she attended New York University, where she obtained a bach-elor's degree in business administration. Returning to Bastalayo, she pursued nursing, while teaching at an elementary school and working part-time at the Bastalayo Hospital Medical Center, where she helped with cancer patients.

Angelina had a passion for teaching and loved children; she loved teaching them and watching them grow; she loved the look of excitement in their eyes when they discovered something new. A love for people was in the core of her heart. She believed in the best of people and would do whatever she could to help a per-son who tried. A full-time position had opened at the hospital, so Angelina took it and started to work only part-time at the school.

"This is wonderful news," said Lucius, "but tell me what about the young man, Mr. Miller—where does he come in?"

She stood up and walked to the back of her grandfather and gently kissed him again on the back of his head; then she put her arms around his neck. "Grandfather, I don't know! I've developed such strong feelings for him. When I'm with him, I am excited and feel safe and secure. He's loving, mysterious, funny, and gorgeous. But he's going home soon, and my life is here."

"Strong feelings? What sort of strong feelings?"

"I'm in love with him, but I'm afraid. I'm afraid he will leave and break my heart. I don't see how it can work. This is not the life for him, and I'm not ready to give up mine."

"Oh, I see!" said Lucius. "So, you are holding back your heart because you do not want to be hurt?"

"Yes! He leaves at the end of this month, and he called me and said we needed to talk."

"If this is true love, things will somehow work themselves out. Just be honest with yourself and him."

"Mother left Bastalayo and moved to New York with my dad, and they were happy."

Lucius was watching her expression as she made that statement. Was she considering doing the same if the question came up? She certainly had to process it all and figure out how to compromise her love, her work, and her life's goals.

"Will you hear the counsel of an old man?"

"Certainly, Grandpa."

"If love is true, it will be patient and unselfish and will give rather than take. I know it is said that people should follow their hearts, but not every heart is ready. For you, you must trust in the principles of love and must take your time and have faith."

"Oh, Grandpa, if only it were that simple!"

"Who said anything about love being simple?"

"You're right. Thanks, I'll certainly think about what you said."

She sat in the chair next to Lucius, and the two gazed out the window, watching the tide come in, while a large white seagull landed at the base of a tropical tree not far from the house. In its beak was a blue tang.

CHAPTER FIFTY-NINE

A black BMW drove down an old and dusty road on the outskirts of Havana. The four men inside the car were sitting quietly. They drove by a small lake surrounded by banana plants.

"Tomaso, pull the car over here; Myron, give me a burner phone that is untraceable," said Romeg.

After stepping out of the BMW, Romeg walked until he was out of voice distance of his three associates. He carefully added a voice distorter to the phone and then dialed an international number to another burner phone. A Colombian man answered.

"Is Papi the only one on the hill?" said Romeg.

"No, there are many others beside him," replied the man, which was the answer to the secret code they used. "I was wondering when you would call," said the Colombian.

"I need your services. I have a big job for you, and this could get very messy. Are you sure this is a secured line?" asked Romeg.

"Don't worry! No one has these numbers," said the Colombian. Both men were careful not to mention real names.

"I want three people dead, and two of them are very dangerous."

"No problem. Do you remember my price for heavy work?"

"Yes. I'll transfer the money today."

"Excellent. Now whom do you want dead?"

"Ambassador Sydney Ballantyne, Sergeant Ed Miller, and the soldier Yolanda Hernandez. Miller and Hernandez are part of a five-man team, but most of the time, they all split up on different jobs, so you can pick them off when they are alone."

"Send me the information, and I will take it from here."

"Good," said Romeg. "You're a good friend; I will not forget this."

"Good-bye," said the Colombian.

Romeg hung up the burner and removed the voice distorter. He tossed the phone into the lake and walked back to the car. The four men drove off.

CHAPTER SIXTY

Detective Williams's old black phone rang loudly. Kaboo was the only one in the office at the time, and after answering it, she heard the voice of Sergeant Miller.

"Detective Kaboo, Second Precinct."

"Hello, Detective. I was trying to reach Wilson. He's not answering his cell."

"He's not in today; he was feeling under the weather. He probably has it turned on emergency mode only. Can I help you instead, Sergeant?"

"I've got something for him that concerns Alicia Ballantyne's car."

"You want to share that information?"

"I've got the name and number of the buyer of the Tesla she was driving. I had my man Rollins confirm it all, and the sale appears legit. The only problem is that the man is in Venezuela, a little way out of your jurisdiction."

"Yeah, I'd say that is a problem, but Wilson has an FBI buddy who may be able to help. How did you come across this information?" asked Kaboo.

"I'd rather not say, but I hope it helps Wilson get the answers he is looking for."

"I'm sure he will appreciate the information, Sergeant. I'll make sure he gets it."

After hanging up, Ed dialed another number.

ED'S PHONE RANG several times before the other person answered.

"Hey you," said Ed.

"Hi you," said Angelina.

Pausing momentarily, trying to find the words to say, Ed felt a knot in his throat and then continued talking. "I need to see you. May I come over?"

"Sure, but what is this about?"

"I just need to be with you. I'll be there in, say, in thirty minutes."

"Okay, I'll be waiting."

Ed hung up, then dialed the number for the US Army's head-quarters in Bastalayo. Private Benjamin answered, and after recognizing Ed's voice, he patched Ed through to Major Lewis's line.

"Hello, Sergeant," said Major Lewis. "It's been a hell of a six months, hasn't it? I imagine you're ready to pack up and get out of here."

"Yes, sir, I think it's about that time."

"I'll need you to come down to HQ sometime in the next few days. We will need a complete debriefing on your six-month operation."

"Yes, sir. Tomorrow will be fine."

"That's all, Sergeant. You're dismissed."

After hanging up, Ed felt the finality of the assignment, and a heavy feeling came over him. He wondered about the relationship he had built with Angelina—would it end when his assignment ended? Knowing that the time had come to confront the issue, he drove to Angelina's home.

When he pulled his steel-gray Challenger into her driveway, Angelina was waiting on the porch. Ed got out of the car, and he felt his face light up with delight when he saw her. She was wearing a soft, short-sleeve blouse that was white and almost see-through, along with white loosely fitting pants that went right below her calves. Around her neck was the eighteen-karat-gold necklace and diamond pendant, the one that her grandfather had given her.

She ran to Ed, causing his heart to leap inside his chest. His feelings for her had become so strong that he found himself in a state of conflict. What he was about to do would be hard, and it would hurt. When she ran into his arms, he started to speak, but she quickly sealed his lips with a finger and then replaced it with a kiss.

"I love you," she said, looking him in the eyes.

"I love you back," said Ed.

"Come inside. Grandpa has gone over to a friend's house; he will be gone until the evening. You and I are alone, and I want to take advantage of every moment with you," said Angelina.

She took Ed by the hand and led him to a couch in the living room. Next to the couch and on a table was a bottle of Mascot, two glasses, and some snacks. The glasses were already full, and after picking up one glass, she raised it to Ed's mouth and slowly tilted it to pour a gentle stream; then she replaced the glass with her mouth and tongue. As we held each other tightly, she softly moaned, which in turn thrust Ed into a deeper sensation, and adjusting her body against his, he placed his hands upon her buttocks and pulled her against his now hardening manhood. She could feel the bulge in his pants, that he was hardening, and Ed felt the stiffening of her nipples, as they embraced even more tightly.

They had not made love, not at the beach or after the magic night at Kwame's club or any other time, but time was running out. Ed needed her, in his mind, body, and soul—as did she. "Babe," said Ed, "I love you, and I want you, but—"

Angelina quickly covered Ed's mouth with her hand. "Don't say anything; just hold me; don't stop kissing me," she said.

Ed picked her up and carried her up the stairs, toward the bedroom. Going through the door, he saw a large bed covered in pink linen, and the two large pillows were of a matching color. After carefully laying her down across the bed, Ed lay upon her, still engulfed and intertwined in a kiss, her hands running up and down his shoulders and back. She was so soft and smelled so wonderful that Ed was becoming lost in her touch. She moaned loudly, brushing her fingers through his hair and down his face, as his body pressed against hers.

Ed began to explore her more, and he was panting in heat. He babbled sweet words to her, his passion blurring his words, as their mouths and tongues explosively danced and entangled themselves. The adrenaline increased, and the sense of vitality was tinged with some sort of aphrodisiac.

Ed's phone suddenly rang.

"Don't answer it," said Angelina, sealing her mouth against mine, breathing the words directly into Ed's mouth.

But it was no ordinary ring—this was an emergency alert, one that Ed could not ignore. "I'm sorry, babe; I have to take this," he told her. Rising up from her, he grabbed the phone and answered it. Angelina rested on the bed, brushing her hand back through her hair, exhaling in mild frustration, waiting.

"This is Sergeant Miller. What's up?"

"This is Major Lewis. We've got a situation: another attack against the ambassador is imminent, and it's coming quick. You are immediately on red alert, so grab your team and secure the ambassador."

"Yes, sir, I'm on it."

Ed looked back at Angelina and saw the disappointment on her face. "Babe, I'm sorry, but I have to go. I'll call you when I get done," said Ed.

"Do what you have to do; I'll be all right," said Angelina.

As Ed left her bedroom and home, he realized that he had not talked about what needed to be said. It would have to wait.

CHAPTER SIXTY-ONE

Rolling down the coastal highway on Hell Fighter, Marrio and Crystal rode in a state of harmonious bliss, passing all the cars in the right lanes. As they cut through the ocean's wind, taking in the vibes of Mother Earth, Marrio shouted, "I love this!"

"Me too! I love this, and I love you!" said Crystal.

Marrio turned his head so that she could hear him. "You do? Well, I'm hard not to love," he responded.

Wearing a bandana of an American flag around her neck, a blue denim shirt, and a pair of jeans, Crystal shouted, "Faster, I want to go faster!"

"Babe, are you sure you want that? I mean, I'm good with it," replied Marrio. Then he shouted at the top of his lungs, "She feels the need for speed!" He twisted the throttle, and Hell Fighter roared and accelerated to ninety miles per hour. Marrio was completely in his element, zipping in and out of lanes. "Babe, I love that about you. I love that your game," he said.

"You bring it out of me," said Crystal. "You're a lot like my dad—you're an adventurer."

"Oh, is that right?" he said and then jokingly blurted, "Who's your daddy!"

"Who's your daddy!" shouted Crystal jovially. "You are the big daddy! You're crazy!" She broke into laughter.

"Yeah, and you love it!" said Marrio.

Hell Fighter roared on, and as they approached thicker traffic, Marrio slowed down, spotting a quaint patch of beach up ahead. He pulled over and drove onto the sand. Driving slowly, being careful to prevent sand from getting in the bike's parts, he found a stretch of flat, solid rock, where he stopped and parked Hell Fighter. They both dismounted her, and they removed their boots and socks and then proceeded to walk toward the water. As they casually walked along the water while holding hands, the tide slowly was rising.

"You really are something," said Marrio.

"I can say the same about you," said Crystal. She reached down and splashed water, hitting Marrio in his face and then took off running.

"Oh, someone is feeling playful!"

Marrio chased her and caught up quickly; he picked her up and spun her around several times before laying her down on the sand, where he spread himself on top of her. "I should hold you here until the tide comes in and drenches you."

"You wouldn't dare."

"Oh, I wouldn't? Let's see...it shouldn't be more than fifteen minutes before the tide comes in. I'm happy to wait."

She was not sure whether he was kidding or not. "You wouldn't dare. Would you?"

"Well, it depends."

"Depends on what?" asked Crystal.

"Depends on how you answer my question."

"Oh? Ask me anything."

"Will you come back with me to San Antonio and meet my family?"

Crystal was taken by surprise. She had not realized that this gorgeous playboy soldier would go there. "What are you saying?"

"I'm saying I don't want this to end."

"You're scaring me. Are you saying you're…" She stopped halfway through her sentence and waited for Marrio to finish it.

"I'm feeling things I've never felt with anyone else. I'm scared too, but I need to know how you feel, and I can't unless I get you out of this fantasy realm. I need to know for sure."

"Know what, Marrio?" she asked rhetorically, wanting Marrio to say three words.

Marrio held back, knowing that if he said the words, he would pass the point of no return. "Just come with me for one week, meet my folks, and see my life and my world."

"Get off me. Why did you wait until now to ask? There is so little time left before you leave."

"Babe, I know. It is something I've been wanting to say, but time just slipped away. My being with you on this enchanted island has been crazy and amazing—so amazing that I'm lost in these wonderful feelings. Come with me, please. *Trust* me."

"Take me home. Now."

As they walked back to Hell Fighter, Marrio reached for Crystal, turned her around, pulled her to himself, and kissed her passionately. After he finished, he said, "Trust me."

CHAPTER SIXTY-TWO

On the same day, two hours into the afternoon, Evelyn Thomas went to meet with John Bryant, a CIA agent. Bryant was a quiet man, but when he spoke, his words were powerful and intense. He carried a lot of weight in the agency, according to Evelyn's inner circle of associates. She had learned of him through some of her associates' political dealings. She perceived that John Bryant had a sinister side and that people feared him.

They held their meeting at a small and obscure coffee shop in the impoverished side of town. She would have stuck out like a sore thumb if she had not dressed to fit in; an individual might think that she had taken lessons from Sherlock Holmes. "God, I hope this works," she said to herself.

At the coffee shop, she ordered a chilled coffee, nothing fancy, nothing that could draw attention to herself; then she sat at a small table at the rear of the establishment. She looked at her watch and saw the time was 2:07 p.m. "Come on, Mr. Bryant. Where are you?" she whispered.

As soon as she made her comment, John Bryant walked in. He was not much to look at: he had a medium height and medium build, and his gray hair was thinning. He had been around awhile, a testament to his ability to play the game well. He sat down opposite to her, and after crossing his legs, he peered out the shop's front window, scanned the room, and then focused on Evelyn. "Hello, Evelyn. A hell of a situation you have here. Who could have guessed it would get this messy?"

"Can you help me?"

"The information about Alicia Ballantyne's car is going to come to light. You do know the whole case was covered up for the greater good. Those big oil companies have powerful, far-reaching tentacles, and they, the oil companies, have the influence to suppress the truth. They have pretty much had their way for a long time now, but Evelyn," he said, pausing to get her full attention, "our knowing what happened was not a problem for us." Bryant looked out the window, waiting for a response from her."

"Oh, I see, but what is it going to take to make this problem go away for good?"

"Your husband has caused a lot of problems over the years. We've allowed him to continue his operations in Africa, those in which he sells arms to causes that often oppose our special interests, but now he has gone too far, trying to assassinate an ambassador on American soil. We can't afford this type of publicity, and our people have grown tired of it. Give him up and whatever you know about Landoza Arms; in return, your little problem will go away."

She pondered Bryant's words: could she sacrifice Romeg to save her own skin? "What the hell!" she thought. "He abandoned me years ago, so why should I be loyal now?"

To Bryant, she said, "I can gather what you want, but it will take some time. Give me two days."

"In two days, I shall be in touch," said Bryant, nodding once. He stood and walked out of the coffee shop. A black sedan pulled up, and he got in and was driven away.

"WOMAN, YOU FEEL so good that I can go again," said Floyd Rochester as he lay beside Evelyn, in her enormous suite in the Dux Chantley Hotel and Resort, which was next to Bastalayo's mountains. Dux Chantley was exclusively for the rich—not by exclusion but by price alone. Exuberant prices guaranteed that only the rich and upper-class clientele could afford it.

"I could use some more spoiling myself," said Evelyn. "Pour us some drinks, and then get back in this bed."

"Your wish is my command. How about a double lucky-lemon seven?" he asked, scurrying naked across the room to the bar.

"Sure, why not?" she replied, knowing she had gathered all of John Bryant's requested information. It was still unsettling that she was betraying the man she once loved and would have died for, but years of being in the shadow of another woman had brought her to this point. She had been frustrated with constantly feeling insignificant and unappreciated by her one and only true love, frustrated that the candle had burned only on one side, frustrated to realize that Romeg had used her only to rebound from Alicia's rejection.

Earlier that day, she spoke with John Bryant and told him everything was ready. She had flown quickly to the Grenadines and back gathering what she needed to free herself for good. There was no turning back now.

"Hurry up! Get back in this bed!" she yelled.

Floyd handed her the drink, which she hurriedly devoured and then rolled onto Floyd and pressed her lips heavily upon his. She actually hurt him, but not wanting to show weakness, he bore the pain and then flipped her over and lay on her. For the second time, he entered her, violently thrusting his body against hers until she climaxed. If she had not been in such a state of passion, she would have noticed that Floyd stopped not because he climaxed but because a bullet had ripped through his back and directly through his heart.

A well-dressed man holding an automatic pistol with a silencer was suddenly pulling Floyd's lifeless body off her. "Where is it?" asked the man, who had a Colombian accent.

"Where is what? Who are you? Oh! my God! What have you done?" she said. She began to cry. The gunman spoke, looking down at Evelyn, "Did you think we wouldn't follow you and not tap your phone? You were foolish. "Tears will not help you. Now answer me. Tell me where the information is, the information you were going to give the CIA agent. Your answer will determine whether you live or die."

She looked at Floyd's body; sniffling, she then pointed to the safe in the closet.

"Open it," said the Colombian.

Evelyn opened the safe and was handing over the documents when a second man entered the room. This was the man whom Romeg called Papi. He looked the documents over and then told the killer to take her. They used the stairwell to exit the hotel, and Evelyn saw that a security camera had been smashed. Below the camera was another body—John Bryant, who lay dead against the wall.

CHAPTER SIXTY-THREE

I t was an early and peaceful morning at the embassy, and the ambassador was quietly sitting at his desk in his office, with the door cracked open. Ed's team was winding down, knowing the replacement team would be arriving the next day. Thornton, Hernandez, and Roy were still watching the twins at school, while Ed and Marrio stayed with Sydney. Rollins, as usual, was at the base, monitoring the surveillance cameras.

The ambassador's receptionist called to Ed: "The ambassador needs to see you and I will be stepping out to run my errands." She ran these errands everyday at the same time.

Ed walked into Sydney's office and found him looking at a picture of his wife, Alicia, and their two daughters. "It has been two years and six months since I lost her; I don't think I have accepted the fact that she's gone. I never completely grieved," said Sydney, his eyes watering up.

Ed only said, "I'm sorry, sir."

The ambassador continued. "My girls seemed to have adjusted somewhat to their mother's absence, or maybe they put on courageous faces for my sake. Alicia was the only woman I ever loved, and I don't know if I will ever love again."

"I can't imagine the pain you've gone through, sir," replied Ed, his heart going out to the important but vulnerable man before him.

Tears fell down Sydney's face, and he turned away from Ed to face a large portrait of the president of St. Vincent hanging on a wall. "You know what, Alicia and I had dinner with our president and yours at the White House just months before her accident. That night was so wonderful to Alicia and me. My president called me after my wife's death and was very comforting and supportive."

There was silence in the room for several moments; then Ed said, "Sir, you called me in—is there something you need me to do?" asked Ed.

No Sergeant, I just needed to talk for a moment. Meanwhile Marrio was checking the perimeter of the parking lot. Something did not seem right. Marrio could not put his finger on it, but his instincts compelled him to report his unease. Ed walked through the building, checking and noticed that the two Grenedine soldiers that were assigned to guard the Embassey front doors were not there. Running back by the kitchen, he saw them unconcious and appeared to be drugged. The only other person working in the building was the receptionist who was out running errands. Ed radioed Marrio, "get the Lincoln ASAP!" We're under attack, and we need to get the Ambassador out of here now. Marrio hurried, "Sir, I have the car ready and waiting. Running back to the Ambassadors office, Ed grabbed Sydney and told him, "Stay close, we're leaving." Looking down the Embassey corridor, he could see several men with guns approaching the building. Leaving out and locking the rear metal door that led to the parking lot behind them, they hurried to the Lincoln. Ed took the lead to shield the Ambassador. As they approached the car door and Sydney was about to enter, a shot rang out. Sydney shrieked and collapsed to the ground.

"Where did that shot come from?" yelled Marrio. He looked around. "There, across the street—on the rooftop!"

Ed and Marrio hit the dirt. Ed slid on his stomach to Sydney, who was not moving. Ed checked his pulse and found it was very faint—Sydney was still alive, just barely. "Damn it! How did we miss this?" shouted Ed, frantically checking all directions for more shooters. The men that had entered the Embassy were not able to take down the metal door and were forced to go back through the front and around the building.

Across the street, another shooter left a building and crouched behind a car next to the curb. The shooter tried to advance, but two quick pops from Ed's 9 mm halted him. A barrage of machine-gun fire pinged off the side of the armored Lincoln. "Do you see the shooter?" yelled Ed.

"He's on the roof of the first building across the street, the one to the left!" shouted Marrio.

"Come in, Rollins—we're under attack! I need eyes on the area, full scan."

"Sir, we've got a power outage; all of my equipment is down," said Rollins.

Ed realized that they might not be the only people under attack. "Rollins, get out of there, right now, and go down to the precinct. Get Detective Williams, and tell him all hell is breaking loose. Tell him to send help, and check the school also."

Rollins took off without saying a word.

"Cover me, Marrio," said Ed. "I'm going to put the ambassador in the car."

Ed kept a fully automatic M15 with extended clips under the driver's seat of the Lincoln, ever since that first attack. He reached in, grabbed it, and tossed it to Marrio. "Go to work, son!" he yelled.

Marrio listened closely to the gunfire, trying to gauge exactly where it was coming from. "I need a decoy, Ed," said Marrio.

"Okay, you ready?" said Ed.

Marrio nodded.

Ed jumped up and ran to a car not far from the Lincoln. Bullets riddled the pavement inches behind Ed's heels as he ran. Marrio gauged right, lifted the M15, and fired, bullets exploding out of the barrel. A man on the roof of the first building fell over, plummeting to the ground.

Ed dashed back behind the Lincoln. "Nice shot, but don't ask me to do that again," he said, looking at Marrio as if he were nuts. "Now we've got to get Sydney in the car and out of here."

Marrio covered him, sending a barrage of bullets in the direction of the attackers, while Ed pulled the ambassador into the vehicle before jumping into the driver's seat.

"Marrio, get in!" shouted Ed.

Marrio hurried and got into the Lincoln through a rear passenger door, and Ed slammed his foot on the gas pedal. The armored car screeched as it rammed into a Ford Mustang parked in its way. An explosion erupted as the Mustang was ripped apart by a small missile that had been launched from an Escalade, which was approaching from Delvo Affairs Boulevard.

Another shooter was in the middle of the street up ahead and firing a semiautomatic rifle at the Lincoln's windshield. Ed looked at the poor sap and said, "This ain't your day." He ran the man down, feeling a series of thuds as the heavy Lincoln crushed the man's body.

Marrio opened the bulletproof panel on the Lincoln's roof, which had been converted from a sunroof to a gunport, and he popped out and fired at the Escalade chasing them. However, there were two Escalades now.

Ed grabbed his radio. "Come in, Hernandez!"

"What's up, sir?"

"Red alert, we are under heavy attack. The base has been sabotaged. Go into battle mode now. Repeat, battle mode now!"

Hernandez flew out of the school, signaling Thornton to take high ground and scan the area. "I'll get the twins!" she said. Racing back into the school, she said to Roy, "No time to explain! Grab the girls—we've got to get them out of here."

A black Hummer like the team's green one pulled up to the front of the area of the school, where Hernandez, Roy, and the twins were coming out.

"You've got company, Yolie," radioed Thornton.

Three heavily armed men jumped out of the Hummer and raced toward them. Thornton pointed his AR-50 sniper rifle. "Okay, time to earn that paycheck from Uncle Sam," he muttered.

Pop! One man fell.

The other two men started to turn around.

Pop! The second man fell.

The third man frantically sprayed bullets at the team and then tried to turn and spray the bushes where Thornton was hiding. This time, Thornton shot once, and Hernandez added three bullets from her 9mm. The man not only fell but flew backward, crumpling like a rag doll.

For a few seconds, Thornton was shocked, for he had not killed a man before but had suddenly now killed three at once.

Hernandez and the girls ran to the team's Hummer, and she put the girls in the back before getting behind the wheel. Roy, however, staggered to the passenger side, and when he got in, he dropped his head and collapsed into the seat, but Hernandez failed to notice that he had been wounded. She was worried about Thornton.

"Let's go, Thornton—time to get the heck out of here," she said.

Thornton leaped over bushes, jumped into his jeep, and quickly took off after the green Hummer. As their two vehicles made the first turn leading away from the school, more shots rang out from somewhere ahead. Thornton saw the assailant and put four bullets from his 9 mm Glock into the shooter, who fell down.

Hernandez looked over at Roy, who wasn't moving; blood was running down from his chest. The girls, terrified, were lying on the floor in the back of the truck. "Roy has been shot," said Hernandez. "I don't know if he's alive!"

"Just keep moving, Yolie. We'll check him when we reach a safe place," replied Thornton.

A few more shots rang out, riddling the front of Thornton's jeep. The front-right tire exploded, causing the jeep to veer off the road and into a sandy lot. Hernandez saw what happened, and she swung the Hummer around and headed back to get Thornton, who had dived out of the jeep and had run behind a fallen tree, which was about twenty feet away from the crippled jeep. Several more bursts riddled the jeep, and Thornton caught sight of where the bullets were coming from. He did not have his sniper rifle, and to hit the shooters with his Glock would require a bit of luck—but at least he would slow down their volleys of bullets.

Hernandez's Hummer flew off the ground when it jumped the curb and slid through the sandy lot, where Thornton was holding up behind the fallen tree. After the Hummer came to a stop, Hernandez reached over Roy and pushed the front door open, and Thornton scrambled in and shut the door. Hernandez floored the gas pedal and sped away, the Hummer spraying sand as it left.

Hernandez and Thornton heard many sirens, which were coming from several directions. The assailants quickly fled. Among the arriving vehicles were Williams and Kaboo in their own vehicle. Hernandez pulled the Hummer over when she saw that help had arrived. Looking behind her seat, she asked the twins, "Are you okay?" Still terrified, the girls only looked up at her and nodded their heads.

Thornton checked Roy and then shook his head in a way that said, "He didn't make it."

Kaboo got on the radio and said, "I'll need four cars to escort these people back to headquarters, and send an ambulance."

CHAPTER SIXTY-FOUR

Ed sped down Delvo Affairs Boulevard. The men in the two Escalades were still firing at the Lincoln, but their bullets were only bouncing off the rear end of the Lincoln. Marrio shot a tight grouping of rounds, shattering the window of the first SUV and hitting the driver. The car spun out of control into the parked cars along the side of the street and then came to a stop.

The man in the passenger seat of the second Escalade pointed the missile launcher out of his window, aimed at the Lincoln, and fired—the missile whizzed by and missed by a few feet, hitting a closed boutique store just beyond the Lincoln's position. "Can we take them out with the Lincolns machine guns?"shouted Marrio. "No, we'd put too many innocent bystanders in harms way, we have to try something else" replied Ed

"Sir," said Marrio, "we will be in deep crap if we catch one of those missiles."

"Yea, I know," said Ed. "I'm going to make a sharp left at this next street—hold on!"

After the Lincoln screeched and slid around the turn, the second Escalade was still on its tail. Marrio fired another barrage of bullets at the Escalade, which bounced off the front glass.

"Shoot the tires out!" shouted Ed.

Marrio quickly re-aimed the M15 and sprayed the tires with lead. The Escalade's tires were protected by steel-enforced metal plates, so the tires withstood the bullets. The Escalade, as if irritated at Marrio's gunfire, raced up to the back of the armored Lincoln and smashed into its rear bumper, causing it to sway erratically and to bump into several cars parked along the street. Marrio fired another barrage of bullets, this time at the passenger-side door, as the gunman with the missile launcher tried to aim again. This time, Marrio hit the launcher itself, causing the man to drop it.

"Hey," said Ed, "we are not far from the ocean—brace yourself!"

The ambassador was still unconscious, lying across the backseat of the car. Ed again floored the gas pedal, just after making a hard right-hand turn onto a street that led to the beaches. The Escalade was right on the Lincoln's back, ramming the bumper.

"Damn! We need to lose this guy!" said Ed.

As they approached a boardwalk and pier, Ed gunned the Lincoln one more time, shouted, "Spray the windshield on the driver's side, and don't stop firing!" Then he turned sharply onto the pier.

Marrio popped back through the gunport and started firing a full and extended clip of rounds at the driver's side of the windshield. The Lincoln was now moving at eighty-five miles per hour, and Ed was blasting his horn nonstop, trying to warn the few people there so that they could get out of the way. The Lincoln reached the end of the pier and crashed through wooden railing. The Lincoln went airborne, sailing through the air, then splashed into the ocean.

Marrio's never-ending barrage of bullets distracted the driver of the Escalade, who failed to realize that the end of the pier was quickly approaching. The driver saw his mistake too late, and he slammed on the brakes to stop the Escalade, but the vehicle could not handle the sudden braking: it turned sideways and flipped, spinning through the air until it plunged into the ocean. It landed on its roof and sank; neither the car nor the gunmen resurfaced.

The Lincoln, however, was designed to float, and its buoyancy brought it back to the ocean's surface. Ed switched its operations to boat mode.

"Smooth move, sir—you must think you're James Bond," said Marrio.

"Hey, that's why they pay me the big bucks," replied Ed.

Ed drove along the seashore a bit until they were safe. Detective Williams had a small convoy of police cars waiting to escort them in.

"The ambassador was shot. We need immediate medical assistance," said Ed to Williams over the phone. Williams then called in a request for a medical team; then he handed his phone to Hernandez.

"How are the girls?" asked Ed.

"They're shaken up and scared, but they'll be fine. Roy didn't make it."

"Damn it! What about Thornton?"

"He's unharmed but somewhat in shock: he took out four guys, which were his first kills."

"I understand. Let Williams's people handle Roy's body for now. I'll call Major Lewis and inform her. I need the both of you to meet me at the hospital; we still have a job to do. Bring the girls because they need to be seen by a medical staff."

ROMEG'S SECOND BURNER phone rang. He and Papi exchanged their usual password.

"This man and his team are very good," said Papi. "They killed many of my men. You must have your own men finish the job, and I am keeping the money to pay for my losses."

Romeg was furious but kept his composure. "You finish the job, or your name will become dung—your enemies will think you have gone soft. I'm sure you know what would happen then."

Papi was reluctant to acknowledge that Romeg was correct; he did know that word would travel fast and that his reputation would be at stake. He could not afford to show himself as weak.

Romeg said, "What's more, you have many men."

"My men have families; I will not send them like sheep to the slaughter."

"At least you did get the ambassador. Are you certain he was killed?"

"My men said he went down and was not moving; that is all they know."

"Okay then, this is what we can do: we will wait for the right opportunity; then I will tell you when to strike. I'll send my men with yours. Meanwhile, keep the money, and I will give you more when the job is done," said Romeg.

Papi agreed, knowing he had to settle this. "And what about your wife?" asked Papi.

"I am sending my man to pick her up, so release her to him when he arrives," said Romeg.

"I am sorry she betrayed you."

"Yes, I am too. Good-bye for now, Papi."

CHAPTER SIXTY-FIVE

Decision

A few days had gone by since the attack. Angelina's cell rang, and upon answering it, there was silence. "Hello? Is that you?" she asked.

"Yes, it's me," said Ed. "I'm right outside your house. May I come in?"

"Sure, come in."

She walked to the door and opened it. Ed was waiting on the porch. He walked in, and they went to the kitchen. Noticing his countenance, she knew something had happened. "What is it?" she asked.

He needed a moment to gather his words. "That coffee smells good; may I have a cup?"

"Of course," she said. She had made it before he called, and she pulled out two mugs from a cupboard and filled them.

"I had a situation this week at my job," he said.

Angelina could tell from the look in his eyes that he was worried over what he was about to tell her. "Whatever it is, we can face it together," she said, seeking to give him a sense of assurance.

"Have you seen the news this week?" he asked.

"No, we have only listened to music and watched movies on our DVD player. Why? Is there something big you were involved in?"

"Yes, something big happened. You know I am military and am defending our country, even here in Bastalayo. My job always puts me in harm's way, but I haven't told you everything that I do because I didn't want you to worry," he said. After taking a moment to sip his coffee, he said, "This is really good. What is it?"

"A special concoction my dad created when he was traveling the oceans as a merchant marine. It's somewhat of a secret family recipe now."

"Nice," he said.

"So, tell me what happened."

"As you know, my team and I were guarding Ambassador Sydney Ballantyne of the Grenadines. We've been attacked several times, and this week, we were attacked again. It was very bad. The ambassador is in a coma at the hospital, and one of my men was killed in the fight."

"Oh, my God! That's horrible. What about your friend Marrio? Is he okay?"

"He's okay. What I am trying to say is that in my line of work, I often face life and death situations. People normally get hurt, and many people need to be killed. I am one of the men that has to do the killing."

"You're saying you have killed men?"

Ed felt the fear of having to reveal this dark side of himself, terrified at what her response might be, thinking how this could be a deal breaker.

"More than I want to remember," he said.

She looked down at the cup that was in Ed's left hand. She placed her hands on Ed's other hand, which was free. He was trembling as he waited for a response. She turned and looked out the glass window, in the direction of the large tree not far from the house.

"I have seen death many times, even here at the beach home. Come here, and look at that tree, at the top of its branches. You can see it now," said Angelina, pointing to a large seagull. It was watching the waters for its next meal. "Many mornings, I have looked out and seen it eating its prey, doing what it had to do to live. Life is vicious and savage all around us; many people are oblivious to such aspects because of how sheltered they are. I see patients in the hospital, and many are war veterans, good men and women that have done things that are hard to live with. And I see their spouses embrace them and love them." She looked at Ed and held his hands, which now were calm and steady. "Whatever you had to do, I believe in my heart you did it all for the right reasons and because you had no other choice."

She gently kissed his cheek and then his lips. Ed put his arms around her.

"My world is hard and harsh," he said, "and I never know whether I will make it home. I'm falling deeply in love with you, but I can't keep your heart safe from the fear and worry I would put you through."

"Shouldn't that be my decision?"

"Maybe, but I couldn't bear to put you through it, just the same. I'm leaving for Philadelphia on Saturday."

She knew this moment had been coming, but expecting it and being in it wasn't close to being the same. "And what about us? Will there still be an us?"

Ed's emotions surged, and his battle-hardened eyes started to glisten with tears. His phone rang, and he let it ring several times before answering it.

"Sergeant Miller, this is Major Lewis. Are you free to talk?" she said.

Motioning to Angelina, he stepped away. "Yes, Major," he said.

"We are moving up your termination date of this assignment; you will fly out tomorrow to Washington, DC," said Major Lewis.

"Tomorrow? What could be so pressing, Major?"

"You can ask them yourself, Sergeant. There are no options here. That will be all, soldier."

Ed looked back at Angelina. "Wow! My departure date has been moved up. I have to leave tomorrow. I'm being sent directly to Washington, DC. Babe, this is all so sudden, but I promise that when I get there and things settle, I'll call you and we'll figure our relationship out. Right now, I have to go."

Angelina was tearing up as Ed walked toward the door. "I won't try to stop you, but I need to tell you that I love you!" she said.

Ed turned back to her, and she ran into his arms. They kissed one final time before he left.

CHAPTER SIXTY-SIX

Decision

Marrio sat in the lounge of the Buerada Hotel, waiting for Crystal to get off work. Regarding the recent attack, he had shared with her as much of the details as he was allowed to. She had listened to the story on the news and was very upset and hysterical, and Marrio was distressed to see her that way. He had fallen for her and wanted to take her home, but he now saw that he had to make another decision as well. Was it time to stop going on dangerous assignments? Was it time to take a desk job and stay put in San Antonio? Maybe it was time to marry and to raise a family and to take over the ranch, just as his dad had always wanted, who thought Marrio had put his life at risk one too many times and that his luck would run out. It could have been Marrio instead of Roy who died. And he wondered whether Crystal wanted to live with him back in San Antonio. Could she give up Bastalayo?

Crystal walked in looking somber and approached him. "Hello, Marrio," she said.

"Hi, babe. How are you?"

"I'm not quite sure, to be honest. I'm not okay—I could have lost you, and just thinking about that terrifies me. I'm in love with you, Marrio, so much that I want to spend the rest of my life with you—but I can't, not like this."

"I understand, babe. I've been thinking about the situation too."

Marrio ordered a rum and coke and asked Crystal if she wanted one. "No, thanks," she replied.

"I couldn't ask you to be with me under these conditions. I was thinking it might be time to quit the missions, but that's no guarantee that our relationship would work out. We are from different worlds," said Marrio.

Crystal's eyes lightened at the bit of hope. "You would give up being a soldier for me?" she asked.

"I think I would, and I'd like to try. I could decline dangerous assignments and take an office job. Or I could run my family's ranch with you by my side."

Crystal brightened further. "If you run the ranch, I will come with you to San Antonio, and we can try to move forward," she answered.

Marrio grabbed her and lifted her above his shoulders, swinging her around. "Ahh yee!" he shouted.

The people nearby looked at them with delight; all of them could feel the electricity coming from the young, loving couple.

CHAPTER SIXTY-SEVEN

After hanging up with Papi, Romeg walked over to the full-service bar in his hotel room, which spread across the wall and to the right of the room's main door. He poured a large glass of Chivas Regal and then added two ice cubes. He drank a good portion of it in one tilt of the glass. Across from the bar, Myron was sitting on a black leather sofa, the kind often seen in the offices of rich lawyers.

"You know what has to be done," said Romeg. "Make sure that it is not your hands on her, but make sure it is handled and painless."

"Are you sure this is what you want, boss?" asked Myron.

"Do not question me." Romeg put out his hand, having Myron hold up.

"Before you leave, dispose of this, and leave no trace. Handing Myron a black briefcase, he said, "had Dugan not been prematurely killed, we would have been able to frame Sydney, by planting this in the Embassy, but with that Batestra women spilling her guts, we could not afford to expose our man in the embassy and use this to scandalize the Ambassador. Oh, how sweet it would have been to destroy his reputation, then kill him also, but I will find another way. I vow it.

Myron nodded, then got up from the sofa, took the briefcase, and walked out of the room.

IN ROOM 207 AT THE BASTALAYO HOSPITAL, Sydney Ballantyne lay in a coma. Right outside the room, Ed and his team were gathered, waiting to say their good-byes to the ambassador, hoping that he could hear them. The replacement team had taken over; it was being governed by a Sergeant Mark Chancellor, a good soldier known for being trustworthy.

"You may go in now," said the head nurse.

One by one, the team said their good-byes, and Ed was the last to go in. "Sydney, I am so sorry this has happened. I would have taken that bullet for you if I had known it was coming. I know I can't change what happened, but I want you to know I did every-thing possible to protect you, and I won't rest until I settle this for the both of us. We know your aide Dupont was involved and we will get him. I pray you can hear me. I know you're a fighter, tough as nails, so fight. You come back to us; I know you can do it. Your girls are safe, and a new team will be watching over them until you get well. The head man is Sergeant Mark Chancellor; he's a good man and a good soldier, I vouch for him. My government is sending me back stateside, but I promise to keep in touch and check in on your family, no matter where I go."

Bending over the ambassador, Ed placed a hand on one of the Ambassador's and said his final departing words: "I have to go. It's been an honor, sir. Good-bye."

Ed had tears in his eyes when he turned and left the room. Angelina was at the end of the hall, waiting for him.

CHAPTER SIXTY-EIGHT

E d and Angelina walked out of the hospital and climbed into Angelina's car. Ed's bags were already in her trunk. As she drove to the Barack Obama Airport, they shared few words. After pulling up to the departure ramp, they got out of the car.

"So, this is it…have you said all of your good-byes?" asked Angelina.

Ed thought about it. "Yes, I spoke not only to my team but also to Detectives William and Kaboo, Kwame, Crystal, and Lucius. My team will fly back with me to Washington. But I need to say one last thing to you." He paused, looking at her, trying to stretch the moment to its limits. "I want to tell you something. I don't want to leave; I don't want to leave you and what we have shared behind, nor can I let go of considering what we could become," he said.

Angelina just listened as he spoke.

"I need you to know that I will be back, and I want you to hold on to something for me until I do," he told her. He pulled a figurine from his carry-on bag, the same one Ed had purchased from Kwame for his mother.

Angelina looked at the man and woman on a beach. The woman was dancing barefoot on the sand, and the man appeared frozen in awe at her presence. The tide rippled up the sand; the moon was full in the backdrop.

Angelina embraced Ed and pressed her lips against his, and they held the figurine between themselves. After they ended the kiss, she whispered, "I love you."

Ed took one last look at her, then spoke "and I love you" then he slowly turned and walked into the airport terminal, she watched him, until he faded into the crowd.

Back at the precinct, Stella Kaboo walked to the window of their office, where Detective Williams stood gazing out. They watched as an American airline flight flew in the direction of the Continental United States.

"Do you think we will see him again?" asked Kaboo.

"Maybe. But you know what? After these last six months, I realized that life is too short and fragile to take for granted."

Kaboo was picking up a particular vibe. Once again, she wondered whether they were having another telepathic moment. Reaching over, she took hold of Wilson's hand. He squeezed, just once.

The End

Follow the Bastalayo Experience:
email: www.simplybrook.com
facebook: The Bastalayo Experience
twitter: twitter.com/@SBFRAZI

www.ingramcontent.com/pod-product-compliance
Lightning Source LLC
Chambersburg PA
CBHW070050260626
47160CB00004B/1160